Samuel Chenery Damon, America Project Making of

Morning Star papers

Samuel Chenery Damon, America Project Making of

Morning Star papers

ISBN/EAN: 9783337024086

Printed in Europe, USA, Canada, Australia, Japan

Cover: Foto ©Andreas Hilbeck / pixelio.de

More available books at **www.hansebooks.com**

Morning Star Papers:

BY REV. SAMUEL C. DAMON.

" The immense Pacific smiles
  Round ten thousand little isles,
  Haunts of violence and wiles.

" But the powers of darkness yield,
  For the Cross is in the field,
  And the light of life reveal'd.".
                    MONTGOMERY, 1826.

HONOLULU :
PRINTED FOR THE HAWAIIAN MISSIONARY SOCIETY.
1861.

"The isles shall wait for His law."—Isaiah xlii : 4.

"The isles shall wait upon Me."—Isaiah li : 5.

"Surely the isles shall wait for Me."—Isaiah lx : 9.

"Go ye into all the world and preach the Gospel to every living creature."
MARK xvi : 15.

"Lo, I am with you alway, even unto the end of the world. Amen."
MATTHEW xxviii : 20.

"I feel confident that, regarded as a mere money investment, the very best investment this country [England] can make, is to send out in advance of either colonists or merchants, Missionaries, who may prepare the way for those who are to follow."
Sir G. Grey, Governor of New Zealand.

"One thing is consummated and settled in my mind, and that is, a full and delightful conviction that the cause of Missions has never held too high a place in my estimation, or engaged too large a share of my attention. This is saying nothing, and less than nothing. *It transcends—immeasurably transcends the highest estimation of every created mind.*"—Rev. Dr. Worcester, First Sec'ry A. B. C. F. M., 1821.

"It is our duty to visit surrounding islands. A missionary was never designed by Jesus Christ, to gather a congregation of a hundred or two natives, and sit down at his ease, as contented as if every sinner was converted, while thousands around him, and but a few miles off, are eating each other's flesh, and drinking each other's blood, living and dying without the Gospel. For my own part I cannot content myself within the narrow limits of a single reef; and, if means are not afforded, a continent would be infinitely preferable; for there, if you cannot ride, you can walk; but to these isolated islands a ship must carry you. Did you know the state of the surrounding islands, how ripe they are for the reception of the Gospel, you would sell the very gods out of your museum, if it were necessary, to carry the glad tidings of salvation to those now sitting in darkness."—Rev. John Williams, (Martyr of Erumanga,) to the Directors of London Missionary Society, 1828.

> "Come, Lord, and added to thy many crowns,
> Receive yet one, the crown of all the earth,
> *Thou*, who alone art worthy."—Cowper.

PRINTED BY H. M. WHITNEY, COMMERCIAL ADVERTISER OFFICE.

GLIMPSES AND GLANCES

AT THE

SIGHTS, SCENES AND PEOPLE

OF MICRONESIA.

I.

PREFATORY.

A FEW glimpses and glances with an observing pair of eyes, will afford a better idea of a place and people than books of travels and voyages written by the most graphic pen. All are not inclined to journey abroad, or if inclined, do not enjoy the privilege of going, hence they must obtain their knowledge of foreign lands, by reading or conversation with those who have seen those lands and communities beyond the seas. Having enjoyed a favorable opportunity for cruising among the islands of Micronesia and catching " glimpses and glances at the sights, scenes and people " of that remote and unfrequented region upon our globe, we propose furnishing our readers with a series of descriptive sketches, or rather extracts from " our log," while on board the *Morning Star*, during her fifth and last trip to the westward.

The nature of our cruise would not allow time for deep research into the origin of the inhabitants, or for historical investigations, although we have not neglected to peruse such publications as relate to those parts of the Pacific, including volumes of former voyages, the journals of missionaries, and books of natural science. We have read with profit that portion of the U. S. Exploring Expedition, by Lieut. Wilkes, relating to the Gilbert or Kingsmill Islands, the voyages of the renowned Kotzebue, to the Radack Chain of the Marshall Islands, and several other works relating to Micronesia ; also Darwin's Voyage of a Naturalist, and Maury's Physical Geography of the Sea. The most readable and reliable sources of information are the *Morning Star*, or History of the Children's Missionary Vessel, by Mrs. Jane S. Warren, of Boston, and the Lectures of Rev. L. H. Gulick, M. D., published in

the *Polynesian*. We began, however, to treasure up stores of knowledge respecting Micronesia, many years ago, as we sat in our sanctum,
and conversed with shipmasters and sailors, who had visited those
comparatively unknown regions. We were accustomed to do this
long before the establishment of the Micronesian Mission. Since the
mission was commenced, in 1852, we have maintained a frequent correspondence with all the missionaries, having been permitted the
privilege of a personal acquaintance with them, while they were *en
route* from the United States to their distant and lonely stations upon
Kusaie, Ponapi, Apaiang and Ebon. It has long been our cherished
desire to visit them, and behold the changes there in progress. Circumstances have not allowed us to carry out this desire until the sailing
of the *Morning Star* upon her last trip, bound thither with the annual
supplies for the mission-families. While making our preparations to
leave, the Hawaiian Missionary Society conferred upon us the honor of
acting as their Delegate.

When starting upon our cruise, the prospect of a change of scene,
and rest from the long continued pressure of professional duties, was
most refreshing to our jaded spirits. We longed for rest and mental
repose; the idea of enjoying rest and repose amid the unvisited scenes
of Micronesia, served to gild the future with dreamy fancies which
we feared could not be realized. In imagination, we pictured many a
pleasant day's sail along the shores of islands decked in the rich and
gorgeous drapery of the tropics, and over lagoons where

>" Life, in rare and beautiful form,
>Is sporting amid those bowers of stone."

We anticipated much of the purest enjoyment from the friendly
greeting and familiar converse with the missionary brethren. Disap-
pointment has not been our lot. The participation has been more
than was the anticipation. The bright fancies of the imagination
have been realized. If now our descriptions of the Micronesian
Islands appear tame and common place, the reason will be that our
pen has failed to give full expression to our ideas, and experiences,
for we have seen enough, and experienced enough to fill volumes
with far more entertaining sketches than we are able to produce. But
we hope not altogether to fail in our attempts, inasmuch as we
merely propose to sketch " glimpses and glances at the sights, scenes
and people of Micronesia."

II.

OUTLINE OF OUR CRUISE.

Leaving Honolulu, Saturday May 11th, at one o'clock P. M., the *Morning Star* pursued a southwesterly course, running before the northeast trade winds. On crossing the meridian, we changed our Sabbath to correspond with that of the missionaries of Micronesia. No incident of importance occurred during our passage to Apaiang, or Charlotte Island, one of the Gilbert or Kingsmill Islands, lying in 2° North latitude and 173° East longitude. We reached the island, Monday morning, May 26th, fifteen days after sailing from Honolulu. We were greeted with a most cordial welcome from the Rev. Mr. Bingham, before our vessel came to anchor in the smooth waters of the lagoon of Apaiang, for this island is one of the numerous coral islands, forming the Gilbert Group.

We remained at anchor for three days at Apaiang, when we started for the neighboring Island of Tarawa, taking with us Mr. and Mrs. Bingham, as passengers, who proposed to visit their missionary associates, Messrs. Mahoe and Haina, on Tarawa. One day's sail brought us to a safe anchorage in the lagoon of Tarawa. Finding the mission families in health, and usefully occupied, we spent three days, including a Sabbath, at this station, when we squared away for the Marshall Islands, touching on our passage to leave Mr. and Mrs. Bingham at their island-home. Running in a northwesterly direction, after a quick passage of only two days, we reached Boston or Covell's Island, as it is known upon the charts of navigators, but now called *Ebon* by the missionaries, who have followed the native authority. This island lies 4° 39 N., and 168° 50 E. At this island we spent four days—including a Sabbath—when we sailed for Strong's Island, Ualan, or Kusaie, lying in 5° 19 N., and 163° E. L. Having light winds we were six days making the passage, hence did not land on that Island, until early Sabbath morning, June 15. On Strong's Island, we were weather-bound for five days, being unable to communicate with our vessel, which was lying "off and on."

Having landed our supplies, and leaving the mission family of Mr. Snow, in health, we sailed for Ascension, or Ponapi, lying in 6° 48 N., and 158° 19 E. We entered what is called the Middle Harbor, lying midway between the two Mission Stations of Kiti and Shalong. Having spent eleven days there, at anchor, and visiting various localities upon the island, we started upon our home-passage, which we made in just forty days, having been compelled by adverse winds to run as far north as the thirty-sixth degree of latitude. During our homeward passage, we experienced a severe gale on the 22d of July, in Latitude 34° 30, and Longitude 166° E. The vessel was "hove to" about eighteen hours. The gale was most severe between 10 and 12 o'clock at night, when very serious fears were entertained for our safety. Our danger was imminent. At the time we were a thousand miles from the nearest land, perhaps nearer Japan than any other habitable part of the globe. By the merciful in-

terposition of God, we were finally permitted to conclude our voyage
in safety, reaching Honolulu, Tuesday, August 13th, and having been
absent just ninety-three days:—

Sailed from Honolulu, May 11th.

Passage to Apaiang	. . .	15 days.
Remain at "	. . .	3 "
Passage to Tarawa,	. . .	1 "
Remain at "	. . . .	3 "
Passage to Ebon,	. . .	3 "
Remain at "	. . .	4 "
Passage to Kusaie,	. . .	6 "
Remain at "	. . .	5 "
Passage to Ponapi,	. . .	2 "
Remain at "	. . .	11 "
Passage to Honolulu,	. . .	40 "
Total,	. . . . .	93 days

During that period, our anchor was dropped six times, twice at Apaiang, once at Tarawa, once at Ebon, once at Kusaie, and once at Ponapi.
We sailed, in round numbers, eight thousand miles, running as far south as
2 ° N., and as far N. as 36 °, and as far west as 158 E. L. thus our
cruise forms nearly an oblong parallelogram upon the chart. Deduct-
ing twenty-six days that we were lying in port, from ninety-three that
we were absent, will leave sixty-seven sailing-days, hence, we averaged
about 120 miles each sailing-day. Our best day's run was 230 miles,
and our poorest three miles, when we were nearly becalmed on our
passage from Ebon to Kusaie.

The pleasure of our cruise, and the benefit derived from the voyage,
we attribute, in no small degree, to the excellent management of Capt.
Gelett, the efficiency of his officers, Mr. Mosher and Mr. Johns, and the
promptitude and obedience of the seamen, six of whom were Hawaiians,
and the remainder, Gabriel Holmes and William Gelett, were Americans. Our steward, cabin-boy and cook, are deserving of many thanks.
On our return passage, the cabin was filled with passengers, including
Mrs. Sturges and daughter, Mrs. Doane and two children, Mr. and Mrs.
Roberts and two children, Mrs. Gelett, Mr. Ashmead, Masters C. Corgett,
and Edward Damon.

III.

GILBERT OR KINGSMILL ISLANDERS, MEMBERS OF THE POLYNESIAN FAMILY.

Proofs are abundant that the inhabitants of these islands belong
to the same race as those of the Hawaiian, Marquesan, Tahitian and
Samoan Islands. In appearance, they most strikingly resemble Hawaiians. There is evidently a mixture of people coming from different parts of Polynesia. Some strikingly resemble the Samoans, or
Navigator Islanders. Not only does their appearance, cast of countenance, form of body, color of hair, eyes, teeth, and other character-

istics indicate their origin to be the same, but also their language and many of their customs and practices.

In conversing with the native missionaries, we asked them, if they found any words which were the same as those used by Hawaiians. They replied that they did. In a few moments, Kanoa, Mr. Bingham's associate on Apaiang, furnished us the following list:

English.	Hawaiian.	Gilbert.
Fowl,	Moa,	Moa,
Forbid,	Kabu,	Tabu,
Woman,	Wahine,	Aine,
Man,	Kanaka,	Aomata,
Canoe,	Waa,	Wa,
Fire,	Ahi,	Ai,
Red,	Ulaula,	Uraura,
Big Fish,	Ulua,	Urua,
Cocoanut,	Niu,	Ni,
Eye,	Maka,	Mata.

This list, we are confident, might be extended so as to embrace hundreds of words. We hope as our missionaries become intimately acquainted with the language, that they will devote some attention to this interesting subject.

We noticed the natives of Apaiang kindling fire, by rubbing two sticks together, just as we have witnessed Hawaiians do the same thing. The natives of Hawaii and Apaiang, carry burdens on a pole in a similar manner. The more familiarly we become acquainted with this people, the more were we impressed with their striking resemblance to Hawaiians, although, as we shall show, many of their customs and practices are strikingly at variance and dissimilar to what is to be found in other parts of Polynesia.

It has been asserted by some writers that the system of tabu did not exist among the Gilbert Islanders. Such a statement is remarkably at variance with facts. The *tabus* of this people are as marked as those of other branches of the Polynesian family. Sabbath morning, June 1, while the people were assembling, for public worship in one of the villages in Tarawa, Mr. Bingham invited the children, who were occupying a house adjoining the council house. They could not enter the council, while they were undergoing the *whitening process*, because it was *tabu*.

It was *tabu* for women to sit down upon the mast of a canoe, when it lay upon the ground.

It was *tabu* for boys, whose heads had been shaved, and over whom certain incantations had been performed, to eat certain parts of the meat of the cocoanut, and also certain kinds of fish. These boys were required to abstain, supposing it would make them brave in war.

Mr. Bingham related an incident connected with one of the council houses in Apaiang, showing that certain women had broken tabu by entering it. The house was purified and cleansed, by offerings.

IV.

COUNCIL HOUSES.

The existence of what have been styled council houses, forms a most striking peculiarity in the political and social organization of society among the inhabitants of the Gilbert Islands. A council house is to be found in every village. We visited three villages upon Apaiang, and seven villages upon Tarawa, and in every village these houses existed. They are built after the same general style of house-building among those islanders, although larger and more substantial than common dwellings. The uses are various to which these houses are devoted. An Englishman residing upon Tarawa called them houses of parliament. An American would style them, perhaps, house of representatives or court houses. When subjects of a political, civil or criminal nature are to be discussed, the people hurry, *en masse*, to the council house. When one king would declare war against another, he summons his subjects to these places. There questions are discussed. The king sits as president of the council. His chiefs and the landholders express their minds. He quietly listens until all have finished, when he will make known his opinion, and that decides the question, *pro* or *con*. No vote is taken.

If a crime has been committed, the people assemble at the council house to hear what the king shall decide in regard to the punishment of the criminal. Death is the most common penalty for theft and adultery. This is the case when the offender is a man of low rank; but if a personage of importance, then he is fined by taking away his lands.

The council houses are the *hula* or dance houses. For this purpose they are brought into frequent use. Companies of strolling and abandoned women traverse the islands, traveling from village to village for the entertainment of "lewd fellows of the baser sort." The dances are performed in the night, and are attended with those scenes of midnight revelry, debauchery and licentiousness, which degrade and debase the people. Married women are not allowed to be present. Would that the same remark might be made with reference to their husbands'!

It is to be hoped that these council houses will hereafter be devoted to better and holier purposes. Already many of them have been used as chapels or houses of Divine worship. When the missionaries are upon their tours, and would gather the people to hear the preaching of the Gospel, the council houses are uniformly the places of resort. We attended public worship three times on the Sabbath spent upon Tarawa, and each time the services were there held. On one occasion we entered the village before our companions had arrived. The little children led the way to the council house, where the meeting was held.

V.

GOVERNMENT OF THE GILBERT ISLANDS.

Each island of the group is under a separate and independent king. He is the head chief of the island, although there are many other chiefs. The inhabitants appear to be divided into four classes or grades, viz :

1. King.
2. Chiefs.
3. Landholders. and
4. Slaves.

The position of the king is peculiar, for while acknowledged as sovereign, yet he receives no tribute or taxes. He rules, in some respects, with the will of a tyrant or despot, yet in others he appears destitute of all authority. He does not maintain any royal state, or keep a guard. The people appear to have but very little respect for their kings, by no means approaching to that obsequious and servile demeanor which is exacted by the ruling sovereign in some other parts of Polynesia.

THE CHIEFS—Exercise authority in their respective villages, and among their own people.

THE LANDHOLDERS—Comprise the great body of the people. All the land is owned by some one. The long and narrow islands are divided and sub-divided into sections, the lines running from the lagoon to the ocean outside. They are very tenacious of their lands; a man is esteemed and holds sway according to the amount of land which he possesses, and the number of cocoanut trees thereon.

THE SLAVES.—Slavery exists in a mild form. The slave is usually a captive taken in war. The master exacts labor. The slave is a domestic servant. The master employs him in collecting cocoanuts, pandanus fruit or fishing.

The political affairs of the islands are far from being in a settled state. Wars are frequent. The people upon one island—as, for example, the people upon Tarawa—are ever ready to wage war with those upon Apaiang. So the chiefs are ever ready to plot for the overthrow of the king. So far as we were able to judge of the present political affairs of the group, they very much resemble the condition of things on the Sandwich Islands previous to the conquest by Kamehameha I. It would doubtless now prove an incalculable blessing if the whole group was placed under some powerful dynasty.

VI.

ROYAL FAMILY OF TARAWA.

Tentebau is really the sovereign of this island, although his grandson, *Tekourabi*, is the acting king. Tentebau is a very old man, probably between eighty and ninety years of age. He has a very numerous progeny. He has seven children, (including five sons and two daughters,) twenty-three grandchildren, twenty-one great-grandchildren, and two great-great-grandchildren. Should the old man live many more years, at the average increase upon Tarawa, his descendants will become very numerous. His family is married and intermarried in every village. The old man has been a famous warrior. His body now bears the scars and marks of many a fierce encounter with his enemies. He says that he has been engaged in nineteen battles. The expression of his countenance very much resembles the portrait of Kamehameha I., hanging in the palace at Honolulu.

Tentaberanau, the son of the old king, would naturally be the reigning sovereign, but in consequence of his total blindness, he has resigned in favor of his son Tekourabi, mentioned below. This is a singular state of things. One person too old to rule, and another willing to resign because totally blind. This blindness is the result of a wound received in battle.

Tekourabi, the ruling king, is about thirty years of age. In personal appearance, large and fleshy, yet apparently a man of great strength. He has but one wife, and several children. In his habits and manner of life, he is a thorough Tarawan, giving himself up to pleasure and the rollicking habits of a "fast man," yet he is a stern ruler when he takes hold of the reins of government; the life of a subject is of but small account at such times. The following instance indicates the manner of administering justice in Tarawa. When Mahoe and Haina were stationed there nine months ago, the king promised his protection. The missionaries suffered from thieves. The king warned the people to beware, but a theft was again committed. The thief was detected, and the king, with his own hand, put the man to death—much to the regret of the missionaries, but without their knowledge. This summary method has put a stop to all annoyances of this kind, so that now the missionaries are living in the utmost personal security.

Should any of our readers be disposed to censure the penal code as administered by the king of Tarawa, let it be borne in mind that not a century has passed away since an English Judge declared, "If you imprison at home, the criminal is soon thrown back upon you, hardened in guilt. If you transport, you corrupt infant societies, you sow the seeds of atrocious crimes over the habitable globe. There is no regenerating a felon in this life. And, for his own sake, as well as for the sake of society, *I think it better to hang*." Those were days when the English penal code made deer-killing, sheep-stealing, cattle-maiming and tree-destroying, capital crimes.

It was our pleasure to see four generations of the royal family of Tarawa present at divine service on the morning of the Sabbath, June 1, when the Rev. Mr. Bingham improved the occasion to speak of the sorrow of the missionaries, that a man should have been put to death for theft, and informed the king that a severe fine, or some other punishment, would be preferable.

VII.

WHAT ARE THE PROSPECTS OF THE MISSION UPON THE GILBERT ISLANDS?

We answer unhesitatingly in that good old Saxon word, *good*. A good beginning has been made. There has a most favorable impression gone abroad. The Rev. Mr. Bingham, assisted by Hawaiian Missionaries, has been laboring for years upon Apaiang. We will now endeavor to state what they have accomplished. They have acquired a correct knowledge of the language. Small portions of the New Testament have been printed in that tongue. Mr. Bingham hopes to have ready for the press at the end of another year, the Gospels of Matthew, Mark, Luke, John and the Book of Acts. A small collection of hymns has also been printed. Some of these are original, and were written by Mr. and Mrs. B., while others are translations of several English hymns, familiar to all, viz:

" From Greenland's Icy Mountains," &c.
" There is a happy land," &c.
" I love to steal awhile away," &c.
" Mysterious Sweetness sits enthroned," &c.
" When thou, my righteous Judge," &c.
" Guide me, O thou Great Jehovah," &c.

Some primary reading books, have also been prepared.

At the station, Mrs. B. and the wife of Kanoa, have each been engaged in teaching a week-day school. Twenty-four pupils have been taught to read, and received much elementary instruction in geography, and other useful branches. It was our privilege to attend an examination of these pupils. The amount of Scriptural knowledge which they had acquired was truly gratifying. Several of Mrs. B.'s pupils would answer questions equal to the advanced classes in the very best Sabbath Schools of Christain lands. It was our privilege to examine yer pupils, as well as those taught by Kanoa's wife, and the wives of the Hawaiian Missionaries on Tarawa. Olivia, the wife of Mahoe, on Tarawa, has done herself great credit. Although she has been at that station but nine months, still she has formed a promising class of pupils. It was a pleasant sight to see Olivia, a pupil of Miss Ogden, thus engaged as a most efficient missionary among the poor and degraded people of Tarawa. The wife of Haina, the other missionary, is a most worthy and exemplary Christian woman, faithfully occupied in her appropriate missionary work. No where has it ever been our privilege to witness three Hawaiian families (Kanoa's, Haina's and Mahoe's) which were better conducted, or more exemplary. They all have children. We think such families cannot but exert a good salutary influence among a heathen people. Would that every island of the Gilbert Group had such mission families living among them.

The work at Mr. Bingham's Station, on Apaiang, has assumed a most interesting aspect. Several give the most gratifying evidence that they are truly converted souls. Two have been baptized. One of these is a remarkable youth, of about sixteen years of age. He has been a member of Mr. B's family about one year, and is actively engaged with Mr. B. in the work of translation. The assistance which he renders is vastly important. After they had collected about two thousand words of the language, Mr. B. offered this young man one dollar a hundred for additional words. He had already gathered about six hundred. In the work of translation he goes over with Mr. B., word by word of the New Testament. Mrs. B. too lends her aid, and when the translation is completed, then she will prepare a neat and beautiful copy for the press. If there be a sight on earth, which we may suppose would arrest the attention of the Apocalyptic Angel, flying through the midst of heaven, having the everlasting gospel to preach, it must be that group of translators upon the lone Island of Apaiang. If it were in our power, we should delight to transfer the living picture to the canvas, with the genius and skill of an Italian painter.

Among the candidates who are affording pleasing evidences that they will ere long become united with the church of Christ, are the King and Queen of Apaiang. They were both at the Wednesday evening prayer-meeting, May 28th. It was our privilege to unite with those heathen converts in prayer, led by the King. At the close of the meeting, the additional privilege was afforded of uniting in the celebration of the Lord's Supper. Could the friends of missions have been present in that assembly, I think they would have agreed with us in the remark, that a *good* work had commenced upon Apaiang—that a *good* beginning had been made among the inhabitants of the Gilbert Islands. and that there was a reasonable prospect that the good work would progress. We entertain no manner of doubt upon this subject, provided the work of missions is vigorously prosecuted.

VIII.

THE REV. MR. BINGHAM'S RETURN TO HONOLULU.

On the arrival of the Rev. Mr. Bingham, Jr., at Honolulu, in 1857, several of the chiefs who had long been intimate friends of his father, and many others, were anxious that he should remain and occupy the post so long occupied by his honored father. They reminded him, that his father, on the birth of the son, promised them that he should be their teacher. But Mr. Bingham, in consultation with his brethren, decided that it was not expedient for him to turn aside from his purpose to go and preach the gospel in " the regions beyond." In 1860, with the full approbation of the Prudential Committee, and of the Rev. Mr. Clark, pastor of the church in Honolulu, whose health and advancing years required that he should be relieved of a part, at least, of the many labors of so important a post, the First Native Church of Honolulu made out a formal call for Mr. Bingham to return and become their pastor. This call was approved of by the Hawaiian Evangelical Association. The call was forwarded by the *Morning Star* last year, but Mr. Bingham did not see his way clear to accept the call, but intimated that he might do so at a future time, under certain conditions.

On the return of the *Morning Star* this year to his station, although the church did not think best to renew the call *formally*, yet the pastor of the church informed him that the door was still open, and the call for his labors was more urgent than last year, referring the whole decision of the case to his own judgment. It is proper to say also, that the subject was again brought to his mind by the Secretary of the American Board in Boston.

As we have just remarked, the call was renewed this year, and we were requested to "second" that call. Before consenting to do so, we were rejoiced that the privilege would be allowed us of going upon the ground and viewing the call from a stand-point on heathen, not Christian soil. On our arrival at Apaiang, the subject was very soon made the topic of conversation, and was thoroughly and prayerfully discussed. But while the subject was under consideration, in company with Mr. and Mrs. Bingham, we called upon the King of Apaiang, visiting the church on our way to the council house, where we met his Majesty. Having been introduced, and the object of our visit to Micronesia stated, with Mr. Bingham as interpreter, we conversed awhile respecting Capt. Handy, bark *Belle*, and other topics; at length the subject of Mr. Bingham's removal to Honolulu, was taken up. We informed the King that the people of Honolulu had sent a request for Mr. and Mrs. Bingham to return to Honolulu, and we stated also the nature of the call. We then asked him what was his "thought upon the subject." After a moment's silence, with a countenance expressive of perplexity and concern, he replied, "If Bingham goes to Honolulu, who will be *our friend?*" In the course of our conversation, he very soon repeated the same remark, "If Bingham goes to Honolulu, who will be our friend?" This suggestive view of the subject led us to be very cautious how we endeavored to persuade a missionary to leave his field, and return to preach in a Christian land. I remarked, however, to the King, "Suppose Mr. Bingham goes, and Dr. Gulick is sent to take his place." He replied that "that might do."

While this conversation was going forward, a group of natives gathered around and silently listened to what was said. We were much impressed with the question of an old native woman, evidently one of the common people. She asked, "Have you no missionary at Oahu, that you came to take ours away?" We could not reply that Oahu was destitute of missionaries. We returned from that interview firmly resolved that Mr. Bingham should not be induced to leave for Oahu through any solicitation on our part. We were not prepared to say, that duty might not call him away from Apaiang, but we did see that he occupied a position of influence, usefulness and importance, second to no other within the range of our knowledge. We saw, moreover, that a missionary and his wife, who have acquired a heathen language, and are usefully engaged in their work, are too valuable servants to be removed from their station, unless for the most important considerations, and under the pressure of the most weighty calls.

It now remained for Mr. Bingham to return a definite answer to the call from the First Church in Honolulu. He subsequently gave us to understand, that he had decided to accept the call, and enter upon his duties next year, provided the following conditions were complied with, viz:

First—The Rev. Dr. Gulick, or some other suitable missionary, be sent to take his place.

Secondly—His honored father should return to Honolulu, and

Thirdly—His removal should not take place until the close of another year's misssonary's labors, when he would have the gospels ready for publication, and other work accomplished.

Hence, on the return of the *Morning Star*, next year, we may confidently expect to see Mr. and Mrs. Bingham, provided those conditions are complied with. Their arrival will be hailed by many with delight, and most surely no Christian brother, could become Pastor of the First Church of Honolulu, whom we should more delight to see occupying that important position, if his present post can be as ably manned, otherwise we hope he may not come. Should this measure be carried out, we shall expect that his influence here will continue to be felt in behalf of the Micronesian Mission, and we foresee many ways in which he may still labor for the benefit of the people of Apaiang. In conclusion, we would add, that throughout the protracted correspondence upon this subject, the removal of Mr. and Mrs. Bingham will not be accomplished through any self-seeking on their part, for we are fully confident that both of them would now prefer living and laboring at Apaiang, rather than in Honolulu.

IX.

SEA-SICK POETRY.

Kind reader, you may have perused what scholars denominate lyric, tragic, epic and doggerel poetry, but we doubt whether any specimens of *sea-sick poetry* ever fell under your observation. During our homeward passage from Micronesia, two of our lady passengers were sadly afflicted with sea-sickness. Their cases were desperate! Not even Jayne's medicines could effect a cure! Perhaps there is no sovereign cure for sea-sickness but that recommended by Punch, who prescribes for sea-sick invalids, "not to go to sea!"

We ought not to omit mentioning the fact, that the "Ode" was suggested by a dream, in which the half-conscious sleeper fancied herself endeavoring to indite a poetic effusion to "an old sail." She awoke, exclaiming :

> " Oh lend me your wings, old sail"—

When her *suffering comrade* caught the inspiration, and penned the ode, to which a reply was returned on the following day.

Ode to an Old Sail.

> Oh lend me your wings, Old Sail !
>   And quickly I'll hasten away
> From the chilling breath of this eastern gale,
>   To the fields of new mown hay.

Oh lend me your wings, Old Sail !
　For here no case I find—
Old sea-sickness, monster grim and pale,
　Seeks all my powers to bind.

Oh lend me your wings, Old Sail !
　I'm weary of lingering here—
My usual sources of comfort fail,
　I'm dismal, sad and drear.

Oh lend me your wings Old Sail !
　And adieu I'll quickly say,
To my *suffering comrade*, wan and pale,
　And hasten gladly away.　　　　　　　S——s.

Morning Star, *July* 30, 1861.

Reply of the " Old Sail."

Do you ask for the wing of an old rent sail,
　To bear you far hence away
To the land where your nights may be free from pain,
　Nor sickness o'er burden the day ?

When the *Morning Star* saw her natal day,
　My canvas was bright and new,
And I hastened her on 'neath the favoring gale,
　O'er the waves of old ocean blue.

Now I lie on the deck but a shattered thing,
　And to hear my doom I stay,
While with pity I gaze on the sea-sick ones,
　I gladly would speed on their way.

Though furled are my pinions and never again
　May be spread to the breeze or the gale,
With hearty good will, I will render my aid
　To strengthen some other weak sail.

So ye who are weary and worn with your voyage,
　And feel that your life is but vain,
May strengthen a comrade and bid her look up,
　And hope still the haven to gain.

When the storm-king in vengeance shall ride o'er the main
　And wild waves threaten swift to devour,
When the masts, spars and sails and the plank 'neath your feet,
　You are fearing may leave you each hour,

Look beyond, where no cloud overshadows the day,
　Where no surges or tempests shall roar,
And lean on His bosom who giveth thee rest,
　When life's weary voyage shall be o'er.　　G——tt.

Morning Star, *July* 31, 1861.

X.

FACTS AND FIGURES ABOUT GILBERT ISLANDS.

POPULATION.—Captain Randell, a cocoa-nut oil trader, who has long been familiar with the islands, and has probably more influence throughout the group, than any other foreigner, furnished the Rev. Dr. Gulick, with the following, as the population of the Gilbert Islands:—

Makin and Butaritari, (Pitt's Island)	2,000
Marakei, (Mathew's Island)	2,000
APAIANG, (Charlotte Island)	3,000
TARAWA, (Knox, properly Knoy's Island,)	3,500
Maina, (Hall's Island)	4,000
Kuria, (Woodle's Island)	1,500
Aranuka, (Henderville's Island)	1,000
Apamarna, (Simpson's Island)	5,000
Nonouti, (Sydenham's Island)	6,000 to 7,000
Taputeuwea, (Drummond's Island)	7,000 to 8,000
Peru, (Francis Island)	1,500 to 2,000
Nukunau, (Byron's Island)	5,000 to 6,000
Onoatoa, (Clerk's Island)	4,000
Tamana, (Rotcher's Island)	3,000
Arorai (Hope Island)	2,000 to 2,500
	50,500 to 54,000

FOOD OF THE INHABITANTS.—With the exception of fish and a very few cocoanuts, the food of the people consists almost entirely of the fruit of the pandanus tree. They eat the fruit raw, and also prepare it for long preservation. It must be exceedingly nutritious. Let no one imagine that the fruit of the pandanus on the Gilbert Islands, is the same hard and impalatable article as that found upon the Hawaiian Islands. There is nearly as great a contrast between the two as between a *crab apple* and a lucious Oregon apple. It is not only nutritious, but must be an exceedingly healthy diet. In no part of the world, have we seen a more healthy community, than we found upon Apaiang and Tarawa, the only two islands of the group which we saw.

COMMERCE.—The only commerce of the islands consists in the sale of cocoa-nut oil for tobacco. The natives in their degradation and heathenism, manifest but very little disposition for trade except in tobacco and fire arms. A Sydney firm has been engaged in the oil trade and it proved exceedingly profitable. As the influence of the mission begins to be felt, a desire is awakening to obtain some other articles in the way of traffic except tobacco. A few are beginning to ask for cloth, knives, hatchets, and other articles. The King of Apaiang forwarded five hundred dollars, by Capt. Gelett, to purchase lumber for a small house. He had obtained the money, as a commission, for procuring oil of his people for the traders. Judging from the two islands which we visited, there is but little to tempt the trader to visit those shores.

CULTIVATION.—The islands do not admit of cultivation. There is literally no soil. The islands are formed of sand, broken coral and shells, with a thin layer of decomposed leaves and other vegetable substances. The number of grasses, trees, and vines is exceedingly small. At very great labor the natives cultivate a coarse species of *kalo*, which they reserve for feasts, not eating it as an ordinary article of diet. All the islands of this group are low, and of coral formation.

APAIANG.—This island is about fifty miles in circumference. Twenty-seven miles of the island is wooded. It varies from one-eighth, to one-fourth of a mile in width. If all the land of the island was brought into a compact form, it would not form an island four miles in diameter.

FOREIGN INTERCOURSE.—The Gilbert Islands were first discovered in 1765. They were next visited by Captains Marshall and Gilbert, commanding the *Scarborough* and *Charlotte* In 1824, the French navigator, Duperrey, visited and explored some islands of this group. The most thorough exploration and survey ever made, was performed by the U. S. Exploring Expedition, in 1841.

In 1844, the whaleship, *Columbia*, Capt. Kelly, of New London, was wrecked on Sydenham's Island. In 1848, Capt. Spencer, of the *Triton*, was very nearly being cut off at the same island. On the same island the *Flying Fox*, Capt. Brown, was wrecked and in 1852, the whale ship *Ontario*, Capt. Slocum, was wrecked upon Pitt's Island.

At the present time, but very few foreigners are residing upon the islands. There is but very little inducement for foreigners to settle upon any of these islands. On Tarawa we found only two foreigners except the Hawaiian Missionaries. These are engaged in collecting cocoanut oil for Capt. Randell.

SOCIAL STANDING OF THE PEOPLE.—They are an exceedingly debased and degraded portion of the human family. They wear but little clothing. Both sexes, until twelve or fourteen years of age, are entirely destitute of clothing. Adults wear but a slight covering; the males tie around their bodies a coarse mat, while females wear a girdle of fringed leaves a few inches wide. We can add our testimony to the truthfulness of the following language of Dr. Gulick:

"They are pre-eminently indelicate and indecent, possessing very little, if any, of that refined gentility found on Ponapi. Many of their customs regarding the dead are abominably filthy and disgusting, such as preserving the bodies for days and weeks, and carefully daubing over themselves the froth or ooze from the mouth of the deceased. The wife will frequently for weeks after the death of her husband continue to sleep beside the corpse, under the same coverlid; and a mother will sometimes carry the body of her infant about with her till it falls to pieces, and then she will cleanse the bones and carry them. Indeed, it is common to preserve the bones, particularly the skull, of the dead, and carry them about, at times carefully anointing them with oil, and even sharing food with them.

"Heathenism is here seen in some of its lowest and most disgusting forms, though it may be said in alleviation that there is little of that deliberate cruelty and none of that religious sacrifice of life found in-

3

many of the groups of the Pacific. Their religious rites differ in no material respects from those already described in connection with other groups. Stones, the incarnations of deities, are found everywhere, some of which are so noted as to be the recipients of gifts of food, and to receive the prayers of certain priestly ones."

In their moral and social condition they are far, very far below Hawaiians. The natives of the Sandwich Islands are a civilized and Christian people, compared with the Gilbert Islanders.

XI.

FAREWELL GLANCE AT THE GILBERT ISLANDERS.

" O soft are the breezes that wave the tall cocoa,
And sweet are the odors that breathe on the gale;
Fair sparkles the wave as it breaks on the coral,
Or wafts to the white beach the mariner's sail."

Before our eyes catch a glimpse of Ebon and our attention is arrested by the Marshall Islanders, let us take one more glance at the dwellers upon the low coral islands of the Gilbert Group. Poets may sing of the charms of a tropic isle, where waves the tall cocoa, and the waves break on the coral; the disciples of Rosseau may discourse upon the happy lot of the savage; but it requires only a passing glance to dispel the poet's dreams and the skeptic's boasts. However much the charms of nature may delight the eye and please the fancy, yet the actual sight of crowds of naked men, women and children, ignorant, filthy, and degraded, is a most sad and heart-affecting spectacle. We envy not the man who can extol the condition of the heathen, who are living separate, destitute and apart from the blessings of Christianity, and much less do we envy those who, from Christian lands, visiting those degraded people, contribute to introduce among them the vices and diseases of civilized society.

Some of the southern islands of the group have been very much corrupted by the demoralizing influence of foreign intercourse. Not so at Apaiang and Tarawa. But very few foreigners have ever lived among the inhabitants of these two islands, or others in the immediate vicinity. There is little, if anything, to tempt the trader among them, except the traffic in cocoanut oil. It is important that the people should have their desires awakened for something else besides tobacco, in exchange for oil. This will be the result as the influence of the mission extends. Already the happy change has commenced at those centres where the missionary's influence is most felt. Let the tide once commence setting in an opposite direction, and the most happy results will speedily follow. We are not sure but it would work beneficially if some of the people could be induced to emigrate to other islands of the Pacific; the reflex influence would be good upon those who remain at home. Guano laborers might be obtained, we think, with but little difficulty. There are islands destitute of inhabitants where the cocoanut oil trade is yet to be commenced; the Gilbert Islanders are just the men to be employed as laborers, in the same manner Messrs. English & Co. employ the natives of the South Seas, at Fanning's Island.

It is no uncommon event for newly arrived Europeans and Americans at Honolulu, to lament the low standard of civilization on the Hawaiian Islands, and prematurely pronounce the missionary enterprise a failure. We only wish such carpers, growlers and narrow-minded observers could come among us, *via* the Gilbert Islands. On those islands is to be witnessed pure heathenism, unameliorated and unsoftened by Christianity. Compared with the Gilbert Islanders, Hawaiians are highly favored, and elevated in their civil and social condition. On returning to the dominions of Kamehameha IVth, we feel that we have once more taken up our abode in a well ordered and settled civil, social, intelligent and religious community. If any of our island readers are dissatisfied with their homes and blessings, we advise them to visit the Gilbert Islanders. Having made such a visit, we are confident every one will say, in the language of the Psalmist, "The lines have fallen unto me in pleasant places; yea, I have a goodly heritage." Another feeling too, we should hope would arise in their minds, akin to that which led Messrs. Bingham, Mahoe, Kanoa and Haina, with their wives, to take up their abode among that people and spend their lives in teaching the ignorant, elevating the degraded, healing the sick, clothing the naked, preaching to all, and guiding inquiring souls to the Lamb of God, who "taketh away the sins of the world."

XII.

FIRST GLIMPSE OF THE MARSHALL ISLANDERS.

"Strange scenes, strange men."

A passage of two days from Apaiang, brought the *Morning Star* to Ebon, Boston or Covell's Island. This is the most southerly of the Ralick chain. Before our vessel came to anchor, scores of the islanders were swarming our deck. At a glance we saw that a new people dwelt upon this group; lively, active, talkative, prying, shrewd and ready to take advantage, unless we were upon the look-out. The Rev. Mr. Doane came off in a large boat paddled by the principal chiefs of the island. We received such a welcome as none but the lonely missionary can give to one who pays him an unexpected visit. Having heard the island news and reported the general items of news respecting the outside world, we left the vessel for a few days' residence on shore. Here we spent from Wednesday evening until the following Monday. During that period our ears were occupied in listening to narratives of interest respecting the people, our eyes were glancing about at the "strange scenes, strange men," passing before us, and our feet were wearied in rambling over the island and reefs. We felt, at first, rather bewildered, for the contrast was great between the dull, stolid, and indolent Polynesians inhabiting the Gilbert Islands, and the Yankee, driving and go-a-head people of Ebon. Having adjusted our mental reckoning, we began to digest and arrange the facts we had gathered, and jot down the impressions which had been made upon our mind. The mission upon Ebon has been most interesting from its commencement. The very establishment of the mission is connected with a series of most providential and unlooked for incidents.

XIII.

ORIGIN OF THE MISSION TO MARSHALL ISLANDS.

When the Rev. Dr. and Mrs. Pierson arrived in Honolulu, in 1855, they made known their wish to obtain a passage to Ualan or Strong's Island, one of the Caroline Group. The following statement made by Dr. Pierson, we copy from the *Missionary Herald* of September, 1855.

"In conversation with a man a few days since, I happened to ask him if he knew of any opportunity by which we could reach Strong's Island during the summer. He replied that there was a vessel in port, engaged in sperm-whaling and procuring cocoanut oil; and as the Kingsmill Group is the region for the oil, possibly he would cruise beyond for whales, and so touch at Strong's Island. Upon this suggestion, I went to see the captain, and asked him where he intended to cruise. He replied, 'Among the Kingsmill Islands.' I inquired if he would visit the Caroline Islands. He said, 'No.' I told him that I wished to find a vessel that would go to Strong's Island. He said that he was not going into that region. He said that the best he could do would be to take me to the Kingsmill Islands and leave me there; and probably in a few months I should find a passage to Strong's Island.

" He then turned and looked at me very closely, and asked, ' In what capacity do you go?' I replied, 'As a missionary.' He looked at me very seriously for a minute or more, without saying a word; after which he said, ' I have a mind to take you to Strong's Island; for I love the missionary work. I want missionaries to be placed on every island in the ocean; and I am willing to do what I can for the cause. Whalers have been a curse to these islands long enough; and I am determined to do what I can for their good, so as to have righteousness and justice established upon them.' After talking with him some time, he said if we were disposed to take a passage with him, and cruise along through the Kingsmill and Radick groups, stopping at some ten or twelve or more of these islands, he would take us to Strong's Island; but it would be three or four months before we should arrive at the end of our journey.

" Captain Handy has been visiting these islands regularly for about seventeen years for cocoanut oil, has become well acquainted with many of the natives, and understands the languages to a certain extent. Indeed, he had lived upon one of the islands for several months. He is very desirous to have missionaries settle upon both these groups of islands, especially upon the Radack and Ralick Chains. There are no foreigners residing upon them; and we might preoccupy the ground, and so avoid many difficulties that come from wicked foreigners who have gained influence before the arrival of missionaries. These chains of islands are both under one king, and all speak one language. The Radick and Ralick Chains compose Marshall's Group of islands. They lic near together, and contain at least fifteen thousand inhabitants. He says this in one of most interesting places in the world for a mission."

After conferring with the Directors of the Hawaiian Missionary Society, Mr. Pierson was advised to engage a passage with Captain Handy. Continuing his narrative, he writes as follows :

" Mr. Damon and myself called upon the captain immediately, but he said that he could not do anything without first consulting his officers. He took us on board, and summoned the mates and steward to the cabin, and told them that there was 'a great talk on shore, and some people wanted to put missionaries on board for the islands.' The first mate said, ' I for one am glad of it. We need a missionary among us ; and I am willing to take them.' Another said, ' Whalers have done so much evil to the people on these islands, that I will do anything I can for their good. I like the plan ; and I want the missionaries to go with us.' The other said that he was very much pleased with the proposition. And the steward said that nothing should be wanting on his part to make us comfortable. Arrangements were then made for our passage. The captain said that he would give me his state-room ; and the first mate said that he would give his to the native helper, who is to go with us.

" The missionary brethren were so much interested in Captain Handy's views, in regard to a mission on Kingsmill and Radack's Islands, that they invited him to meet them, and give them more definite information. To this he cheerfully assented, and brought his chart along, and gave them a very full description of that part of the seas, the state of society, the manners and customs of the people on the different islands. All were very much interested in his account, and felt convinced that the time had come when these islands ought to be occupied by missionaries. We are filled with joy that our blessed Lord and Saviour has provided such a favorable opportunity for us to explore lands that have never hitherto been visited by a missionary."

XIV.

REV. DR. PIERSON AND CAPT. HANDY, PEACEMAKERS.

The cruise of the bark *Belle*, forms an important era in the bloody history of the inhabitants of the Marshall Islands. The *Belle* sailed from Honolulu, May 24th, 1855, having Dr. and Mrs. Pierson on board as passengers. Nearly a year elapsed before any intelligence was received respecting the vessel. A brief sketch of Dr. Pierson's explorations, will be found in the *Friend* of June 12, 1856. From that sketch we copy as follows : " After leaving the Kingsmill Islands, the *Belle* cruised among the Mulgrave Islands. The islands have been explored but little, upon some of them probably no white man ever landed. Capt. Handy made arrangements for opening a trade with the people ; which afforded our missionary party an excellent opportunity for exploration. A royal party, consisting of Her Royal Highness the Princess Nemaira, her husband, and five attendants, took passage on board the *Belle* and cruised about for several days. The natives expressed a strong desire to have missionaries located among them, and the King promised his protection. Dr. Pierson is hoping ere long to return and commence a mission there." It was our privilege to meet Nemaira, the Princess mentioned in the above extract. She is a niece of Kaibuke, who is of so much importance among the Marshall Islanders, and whose character we have elsewhere sketched.

During that cruise, Capt. Handy, who had obtained a tolerable acquaintance with the Ebon language, exerted his influence, in conjunction with that of Dr. Pierson, to persuade the chiefs to desist from their bloody policy, which had hitherto governed them in their intercourse with foreigners. The chiefs promised Dr. Pierson and Capt. Handy, that they would not cut off any more ships, or put any more foreigners to death who might chance to be cast upon their shores. We are most happy to report, that so far as we have been able to ascertain the facts, the chiefs have scrupulously kept their word. This fact should surely be set down to their credit, and serve to soften our judgment in regard to this people. In justification of their bloody policy and excuse of this treatment, the chiefs set up the plea of the illtreatment which they had received from foreigners. Dr. Pierson, in his report of the cruise of the *Belle*, remarks as follows :

" There are no whites on these islands at present, and no white man has ever lived on any of them for any length of time. The natives have generally shown a hostile spirit to foreigners. Several vessels have been cut off, and a great number of foreigners killed at different times. The reason given for this conduct is, that when *the king* (Kaibuke) was a young man, a (whale) ship visited Ebon, and a native stole something, which gave occasion for disturbance. A general attack was made by natives and many were killed,—among them Kaibuke's, oldest brother, and he (Kaibuke) received a wound in the arm from a spade, which we saw. He declared that he would have revenge, —that he would kill all the whites he could, and cut off a vessel if possible. His order to this effect has never been revoked until recently." See *Missionary Herald*, for March, 1858.

While we rejoice that the chiefs should have chosen to pursue a different policy, and follow wiser counsels, who can withhold his admiration of the mild and peaceful mission of Dr. Pierson and Capt. Handy? Would that all shipmasters, and especially all masters of whale ships, had pursued a similar policy to that of Capt. Handy, towards both the natives and missionaries. Now that Capt. H. has probably retired from the toils, perils and anxieties of a sea-faring life, it must be to him a source of unspeakable satisfaction, that during his last voyage among the savages of the the Marshall Islands, he initiated a policy of good will and kindness towards foreigners in the place of their former cold-blooded and murderous practices; and to Dr. Pierson, who was compelled by the sickness of wife, to retire from his field of labor among this people, it must be a source of the purest joy, that his labors as the pioneer missionary, were not in vain, but that now a plentiful harvest is being gathered from the gospel seed which was sown by his hands.

In referring to the efforts of Dr. Pierson and Capt. Handy, it would be unbecoming, as well as unjust, not to acknowledge the influence and mild persuasion of Mrs. Pierson. Her influence with Nemaira, the sister of Kaibuke, was very great. She formed an attachment for Mrs. Pierson, which still remains, and no opportunity is lost to make inquiries for this missionary lady and first white female who ventured to risk her life among the savages of the Marshall Islands. Her mission was a noble one, and although ill-health [compelled her early to retire from active missionary labors among that people, she may in her home among the people of California, cherish the gratifying reflection, *that having done what she could and all she could*, her influence is still felt in curbing the violent passions, and checking the savage ferocity of men who had previously imbrued their hands in the blood of many who had been unfortunately cast upon their shores. " Blessed are the peacemakers."

XV.

FORMER INTERCOURSE OF FOREIGNERS WITH THE MARSHALL ISLANDERS.

Some facts have already been published, and others are now being discovered, which show that the Marshall Islanders have imbrued their hands in the blood of many strangers and seamen, who have visited their islands. We hope that a new era has dawned upon those benighted islanders. If the mission established upon Ebon has done no other good, we trust that it has effectually stayed the effusion of blood and the cruel murder of any unfortunate mariners who might be driven by stress of weather, or other causes, to seek safety among the people of the Marshall Islands.

The following list of murders and massacres, will suffice to show that the time has come when an end should be put to such bloody transactions.

In 1834, Capt. Dowsett, mysteriously disappeared at the Piscadores, one of the most northerly islands of Ralick Chain. We still hope as the missionaries extend their work northward, that they will be able to ascertain something more definite in regard to his fate. We express this opinion, because the islanders have hitherto been very cautious about speaking of former transactions with foreigners. As one and another joins the mission party, facts are being revealed in regard to the past history of foreign intercourse.

In 1845, Capt. Cheyne, of the *Naid*, had trouble with the dwellers upon Ebon, and one man was killed upon the spot, besides the nephew of the highest chief of the Ralick Chain was wounded and died soon after landing.

Dr. Gulick, in his lectures, refers to a whale ship that was nearly cut off, at Namarik, (Baring's Island) about the same time, (1845), and also two whale boat's crews came ashore and the crews were all killed at Ebon.

During our visit to Ebon, we also heard the story of a boat's crew which landed upon Ebon, some years since, who had plenty of money. A servant woman in the employ of Mrs. Doane, tells this story : When she was a little girl, a boat came to Ebon with six men in it. They had plenty of food in the boat but came for water. Three of the men had on white shirts, and were large, good looking men, not sailors. They had money in a Hingham box or bucket. They had small knives in their pockets. They were all killed by the natives. Their boat was destroyed. Their clothes were put out of the way. She saw them lying together on the ground after they were killed. Their bodies were subsequently put out of the way. The natives threw gold pieces about, and of some they made fish hooks. From the age of this woman and the particulars which she has stated, we are led to suppose this boat may have belonged to the ill-fated brig *William Neilson*, Capt. Weston, who was accompanied by Capt. Dominis and Commissioner Brown as passengers. It is by no means unreasonable to suppose that the brig may have struck upon some one of the innumerable reefs of this part of the Pacific.

From the *Friend* of May 15, 1847, we copy the following paragraphs :

"THE MISSING BRIG WM. NEILSON.—This vessel left the port of Honolulu, August 5, 1846, for China, expecting to return as early as Christmas. Fears have been for months entertained respecting her fate, but conjecture has inspired the hope that she was not lost; perhaps, she might be sold or otherwise detained. The 'Mary,' which left China, March 2d, reports that up to that date no intelligeace had been received respecting her. We can with difficulty bring our mind to the conclusion that all on board have perished and not one survives to report the story of her disaster. There is the possibility, that like the brig 'Express,' the 'Wm. Neilson' may have been wrecked on that some of the numerous islands in that part of the broad Pacific. It is reported however, that a succession of terrible gales and typhoons was experienced in that region of the ocean during the months of September, October and November. Ex. U. S. Commissioner, Brown, and Capt. Dominis, passengers, and Capt. Weston commanding the brig, are removed from their families, which will not soon cease to mourn the absent husband and father, while a wide circle of friends and relations will deeply sympathize with the bereaved. No person in our community was more generally esteemed for his many excellencies as a neighbor, friend and citizen, than Capt. Dominis, and his family have met with an irreparable loss.

"During Mr. Brown's long residence at the islands, he gained many friends, and his private character, we believe, to have been above reproach. There are many in this quarter of the world who will sympathize with his deeply afflicted family. There are many here, who will also sympathize with the family of Capt. Weston. On a former voyage Mrs. Weston accompanied her husband to our shores, when he commanded the ship Congaree. In addition to the above mentioned individuals, it becomes our duty to record the names of others belonging to the ship's company, viz : Mr. George Brown, Junior, passenger ; Mr. Charles Green, a passenger, belonging to Barnstable, Mass. He came to the islands as Capt. Dominis' 1st officer, on board the schooner Swallow. One Chinaman and five Lascar sailors were also passengers.

"Belonging to the crew of the brig, were the following : 1st officer, Mr. Hammet, Martha's Vinyard; 2d officer, Mr. Benson, Baltimore, Md. Seamen, Seth I'. Peterson and Amherst Peterson, brothers, belonging to Marshfield, Massachusetts. David Mann and Walter Tybu, both belonging to Hanover, Mass. The names of cook and steward, we are unable to learn. Two seamen, John Pitts and J. Gilbert, were discharged sick at this port, just before the sailing of the vessel.

"The vessel, we are informed, was insured, as well as the whole, or a part of the cargo, $22,000 in specie."

In October, 1852, the schooner *Glencoe* of San Francisco, was burnt and crew murdered by the inabitants of Ebon. In this affair the chiefs took no part, for they were absent from the island. The *Glencoe* anchored near the anchorage ground where the *Morning Star* lay in safety during our visit, and where we enjoyed the most friendly intercourse with the people.

A short time after the bloody affair of the *Glencoe*, it is reported that a brig touched at Ebon, and active preparations were made by the chiefs and people to take the vessel and murder all hands. Just as the vessel was about to drop her anchor, the wind veered and the master of the brig concluded it unsafe to anchor. Thus the vessel escaped, in a manner most providential. The vessel would have anchored where the *Morning Star* lay, while we remained at Ebon.

In December, 1852, (two months after the sad affair of the *Glencoe*,) the *Sea Nymph*, of San Francisco, Capt. McKensie, was cut off at Jaluit or Bonham's Island. The only survivor of Capt. McKensie's crew, was brought to Honolulu about three years ago. The hull of the vessel is now to be seen in the spot where she was burnt and sunk by the natives. Dr. Gulick reports the *Sea Nymph* as belonging to San Francisco, but unless we are much mistaken, she was under the British flag.

During our visit to Ebon, we also heard of a large ship which went on shore at Bikini, one of the most northern islands of the Ralick Chain. Report says that the ship's company embarked in their boats, but left plenty of articles on the ship, and among other things left behind, was a black New Foundland dog, which the natives rescued, and which is now reported to be among the islanders. We could not ascertain the name of the ship, or the year when the wreck occurred. We hope yet to learn additional particulars in regard to this wreck.

It seems somewhat remarkable that the foregoing facts have not attracted the attention of either the British or American naval commanding officers upon the Pacific Station. From facts which came under our notice while at Ebon, we are confident that the chiefs are fearful that even yet they may be called to account for some one of the many bloody deeds which have been perpetrated within their dominions. The retributive punishment, which a man-of-war might inflict, conveys a terror to their minds. A man-of-war they have never seen, but the name is familiar to their ears. It may seem strange, but it is nevertheless true, there are many islands, even groups of islands, in the Pacific, as yet unvisited by either an English or American vessel of war. We do not plead for the visit of vessels-of-war to the Marshall Islands, for the protection of the missionaries, or because we have lost our faith in missions, but for the protection of commerce and the lives of wrecked mariners. We believe the time has come when it would be feasible to form a treaty with those people. The chiefs, through the interpretation of the missionaries, could be made to understand the nature of treaty-stipulations. Should a vessel of war visit those islanders, they could be made to understand that, should further massacres and murders occur, they would be held responsible. We can readily see that such a visit might be productive of incalculable good. A judicious commander ought however to be selected for the purpose, otherwise more evil than good would be the the result.

We are not ignorant of the fact that an American vessel of war, the schooner *Dolphin,* Lieut. Percival, once visited Mili, or Mulgrave Island, which is the most southern of the Radack Chain. The occasion of that visit (1825) was for the purpose of rescuing a portion of the crew of the American whaleship *Globe,* on board of which a mutiny had occurred. The *Morning Star* has visited that island, and the spot was pointed out where the *Globe* anchored. The mutineers were killed by the natives in consequence of their cruel treatment of the females. The *Dolphin* was upon her return passage from the Mulgraves, when she touched at Honolulu, and those disgraceful scenes occurred, which gave Lieut. Percival an unenviable notoriety, and prevented him from obtaining the command of another vessel for nearly twenty years. He still lives, and in his old age doubtless regrets the mad freaks of his youth.

We should seriously deprecate the consequences if a vessel of war should be sent to call the islanders to account for the past, for we are not sure but in most instances, there may have been injury and insult inflicted upon the islanders, before they were led to lift the murderous knife. Let " by-gones be by-gones," but for the future let there be a fair and full understanding that if new murders are committed, the perpetrators will be held to a strict account. Such a policy would exert a most beneficial and salutary influence. The chiefs are now haughty and overbearing, and voyaging about in their big war canoes or proas, imagine that they are above law, and hence are lawless. The missionary may teach the people the gospel and thereby accomplish incalculable good, but he cannot do every thing. The following facts however, will show that he can work with spiritual weapons when threatened with carnal. On a certain occasion, a haughty and overbearing chief, told the missionary that it was " Ebon fashion,' when foreigners conducted in a manner not to please the chiefs, that they put them out of the way, or in other words, acted upon the principle, that " dead men could tell no tales." This was Ebon fashion. Now the missionary wished to show this proud and lawless chief, what was the Christian fashion of treating one's enemies ; so he conducted the chief into his study, and knelt down and prayed for him and his people. For writes the apostle Paul, " the weapons of our warfare, are not carnal, but mighty through God to the pulling down of stony holds." We have more faith in the prayers and teachings of the missionary,to christianize and civilize the rude and savage Marshall Islanders, than in commerce or warships. Let the missionary and school teacher go among them with a translation of Webster's spelling book, and the New Testament, and the most happy results may be looked for; children taught to sing

" There is a happy land."

we do not believe will grow up to become murderers and pirates.

XVI.

KAIBUKE.

This is the name of one of the most remarkable personages we met at Ebon. He is sometimes spoken of as the King, but that is however far from being true. He is not even so high a chief as some others, or even his elder brother. On one occasion both he and his brother visited Mr. Doane, and we saw Kaibuke, take a seat on the opposite side of the room, thus paying marked deference to that elder brother. He is nevertheless an important character among his people, and upon his word depends the life or death of the people. We could not learn, as there was really any person who could be officially denominated as His Majesty, or His Imperial Majesty, or the President. The government of the islands is in the hands of a body of haughty, imperious and unscrupulous chiefs, whose caprices and whims are the laws of their dominions. Among these chiefs, Kaibuke has gained an ascendancy and influence, in consequence of his energy, tact, impudence and adroitness. He is a complete politician, placed in a position to carry his measures by force, if they cannot be promoted by mildness. He is exceedingly jealous of the teaching of the missionaries, yet has always maintained a friendly intercourse with them. This must be said to his credit, that he has always kept his word that he originally made to Dr. Pierson, that he would protect the mission. He took Dr. Pierson for "his son," and Mr. Doane, "his friend," which is an expressive method of speaking in the language of Ebon. It is also in his favor, that when the *Morning Star* first entered the lagoon of Ebon, in 1857, he, aided by another high chief, prevented her being run ashore and pillaged, as no doubt some of the chiefs and many of the natives intended should have been her fate.

Kaibuke occupies the position of Prime Minister or Secretary of State, although such terms are foreign to the Ebon dialect. He was at church the Sabbath morning we spent at Ebon. The question was asked him in the presence of the audience if he would protect additional missionaries, if they were sent to Ebon. He gave us his word that he would.

We could relate many stories which were told respecting his duplicity, cruelty and lack of trust worthiness, but we prefer to allow our readers to remain in ignorance of the dark side of his character. Kaibuke is no doubt more or less implicated in some of those deeds of blood which have been perpetrated upon the Marshall Islands. We hope however better things for him in time to come. Those who have gone thither as teachers have not failed to point out to him the better way, or that the eye of Jehovah is continually upon him, and that he will be held responsible by the King of kings.

Kaibuke, takes his name from that of a ship, in the language of New Zealand. Several years ago a ship from the "south seas" visited the islands. The ship was called Kaibuke, so he took that name. Another chief took the name of Capt. Terry, from the name of the commander of the vessel.

We visited Kaibuke's residence, and found him surrounded by his wives, (of whom he has four,) and his eleven children, most of whom could not be said to be encumbered with a superabundance of clothing. He is a man apparently about fifty-five years of age, with a countenance indicative of energy and good nature, although not of nobleness and magnanimity. We account him however a remarkable man, and if not too old to learn, we hope to hear better reports of him hereafter.

The following incidents may serve to illustrate the character of this Ebonite politician and Prime Minister. On our first interview, a surprising intimacy and familiarity was manifest on his part. Mr. Doane introduced us as "the missionary at Oahu, to foreigners and seamen." Kaibuke replied, "Mikinari Oahu, Mikinari very good." His eye caught our black coat. He took hold of the sleeve saying, "Me like very good." Remembering the precept that "He that hath two coats, let him impart to him that hath *none*," we gave to it a literal interpretation. Various were the interviews which we had with this Ebon official. Sometimes we conversed upon matters grave and solemn, and at others we carried on trade in a small way, i. e. exchanging fish hooks and jack knives for the curiosities of the country. At the interview alluded to above, when we called at his residence, it so happened that after a long walk, we were exceedingly thirsty, hence we asked for a little water. He said, "will you not have a cocoanut." We assented, of course. One of his attendants was immediately sent off and up one of those gracefully waving trees adorning the coral islands of Micronesia. Soon the cocoanuts were brought, one for each of us present. We passed ours to His Excellency, but he declined. When we all had quenched our thirst, Kaibuke very politely intimated that a fish-hook apiece would be acceptable for the nuts. We (including our two companions) paid His Excellency, Kuibuke, three fish hooks for three cocoanuts, and took our departure. We only mention this fact as an illustration of Kaibuke's remarkable character! If hereafter, in the progress of learning, he should ever acquire a knowledge of the English language, and these remarks upon his character should fall under his eye, he may be assured that "the missionary at Oahu" has followed Othello's parting injunction,

"And naught set down in malice."

XVII.

ORIGIN OF THE MARSHALL ISLANDERS.

Much has been said and written about the origin of various inhabitants scattered over the islands of Polynesia. Whatever theory may be formed respecting Hawaiians, Tahitians, Samoans, or Kingsmill Islanders, we are confident but one opinion can be true respecting the Marshall Islanders. They are unmistakably of Japanese extraction. We know that in making the assertion, we are at variance with the opinions of some ethnological writers. Whoever saw the Japanese embassy visiting the United States in 1860, and the Marshall Islanders, would say that they were sprung from the same original stock. Their features and physical organization are most strikingly similar. We could not discover one Polynesian trait, feature or habit among them. Like the Japanese and Chinese, they are remarkably industrious. They are constantly at work, whether upon the land or sea. They have a saying "Ebon people never tire." This trait is most strikingly in contrast with all the Polynesian tribes, so proverbially indolent.

The Japanese Princes are accustomed to traverse the empire, with large retinues, and thousands of retainers; the Marshall Islanders perform similar journeys upon the sea. Every year the chiefs of the Marshall Islands make long voyages, from island to island of the group. We were so fortunate as to meet the entire company of the chiefs of the Ralick Chain of islands, at Ebon. They were about fitting off for a summer cruise to the north. Their large war canoes were hauled upon the sand beach. On the day of our arrival, there had been a race of canoes across the lagoon. We were informed that thirty large proas or war canoes, would form the expedition north, manned by five hundred followers of these chiefs, who voyage in royal state. These proas are propelled by a large triangular sail, which is so hung upon the mast that it will propel the proa either way. Their arrangements for a rudder, is a paddle fastened by a rope, and which can readily be changed from one end of the proa to the other. They never propel these proas by paddles, but trust altogether to the winds.

In subsequent investigations, it will be interesting to ascertain if there are not strong affinities between the Japanese and Ebon languages. We are not prepared to hazard even an opinion upon this subject, but still the thought has arisen in our mind, from reading the Rev. Mr. Doane's remarks upon "The Ebon and Ponapi Dialects Compared," published in the *Friend* of Feb. 1860, that when a similar comparison shall embrace the Japanese language, that will be found to be the basis of both the Ebon and Ponapian dialects. There is no surer method of tracing the migration of nations and tribes over the continents, islands and oceans of our globe, than by ferreting out the roots and radicals of their languages. In glancing an eye upon a good map of the Pacific, it will appear that the Marshall and Caroline Islands are separated from the Japanese Islands by a breadth of ocean which might be passed over by junks drifting away from land. In looking at the present condition, customs and habits of the Marshall Islanders, we see no great disimilarity between them and the Japanese, which might not have arisen from their isolated and insular position.

In further confirmation of this opinion that the Marshall Islanders are an offshoot of the Japanese, we would refer to their religious opinions. They do not worship idols, but hold their ancestors in great veneration. They have their consecrated groves and sacred spots. Superstitious or religious ideas do not appear to have had a very strong hold upon their minds. Mr. Doane remarked to us, that they were almost atheists. Who does not rejoice that they now are to have made known to them a knowledge of the one only true God?

XVIII.

CHEERING PROSPECTS OF THE EBON MISSION.

From our knowledge of the Marshall Islanders, knowing them to have been extremely hostile to foreigners, as much so as the Japanese, and in all respects so unlike Polynesians generally, we were not prepared to witness much encouragement to prosecute the mission. This mission was first established by Messrs. Doane and Pierson, in 1857. There have never been but two mission-families at the same time upon the island. Dr. Pierson left on account of his wife's sickness, at the end of his second year's labor. Dr. Gulick and family remained there but one year, and at present the Rev. Mr. Doane and Mr. Aea, the Hawaiian Missionary, are occupying the field.

The gospel has made a decided impression upon the people. Preaching is regularly maintained at the station, and upon an islet on the opposite side of the lagoon, to which station Mr. Doane goes every Sabbath afternoon. Mr. Aea teaches a station school and visits two islets for teaching schools, once a week. His services are invaluable. He has now been upon the island only nine months, yet he speaks the language with fluency, and is daily perfecting himself in speaking and writing. He began to address the people when he had been there but three months. We visited his school. When calling the roll of eighty pupils, forty-three answered to their names. We heard them read, saw them write, and witnessed their ability in ciphering. Their progress was really commendable, considering that not yet four years have elapsed since the missionaries began to reduce the language to a written form. It must be borne in mind, that there are no reading or school books in the Ebon dialect, but what have been prepared and even printed by them, upon a little miserable hand press, that would not be worth in New York five dollars. Mr. Doane and Aea work at type-setting and the press, never having been iniatiated into the mysteries of a printing office before going to Ebon. They have printed at this station an elementary book for children learning to read, a few of the first chapters of Matthew, and a small collection of hymns. Some of these were written by Dr. and Mrs. Pierson, who are now in California. With these few meagre helps, these missionaries are rapidly teaching the children and adults of Ebon and the neighboring islands to read. In all their instruction they mingle scriptural truth in every variety of form. It was exceedingly surprising to witness the readiness with which the pupils in the day and Sabbath schools, answered the questions addressed to them. There was a sprightliness, activity, aptness and quickness of perception which gave the pleasing evidence that the youth of Ebon would not fall behind the youth of other and more favored lands, if they could only enjoy similar advantages. The missionaries have certainly secured a hold upon the rising generation which promises a rich harvest in future years.

Not only have the youth of Ebon afforded gratifying evidence of becoming good scholars, but several have already become, in the expressive language of the islanders, "lovers of Jesus." Christians are styled "lovers of Jesus." We met some of these young people, and surely it afforded a joy which words cannot express, to witness their meek and gentle demeanor, and hear Mr. Doane speak of their humble, and consistent walk. One of these may be said to have met a martyr's death, for he was cruelly put to death by a company of revengeful chiefs, urged onward by hatred and passion, and the lying tongue of a base woman. We were assured that hatred of the young man's Christian principles had no small influence in hastening forward his death. May the blood of the martyr prove the seed of the church, in this, as it has in numerous other instances.

This leads us to remark that, while the truth is manifestly and rapidly making progress upon Ebon, among the common people, there are those who are decidedly opposed to the movement. Many of the high chiefs, although apparently upon good terms with the missionaries, are at heart inimical to the preaching of the gospel. These persons tolerate the mission, because, indirectly, it brings ships and trade to their islands ; beyond this, they are exceedingly suspicious of the work which has commenced among their hitherto secluded islands. There are two opposing parties, and the present indications are, that ere long there will be a mighty struggle for the supremacy. It would be no surprising thing if the mission should be violently opposed by a powerful body of the chiefs, who look with a jealous eye upon the fact that their subjects are learning to read and acquire knowledge. These chiefs are keen and shrewd men, and foresee that with the increase of knowledge among the commoners, will arise a party to oppose the old and cruel practices of the rulers of the land. Only upon a much smaller scale, the same elements are at work among the inhabitants of the Marshall Islands, which were at work among the Romans and other ancient nations in the early ages of Christianity, when the Apostles went forth in obedience to the Saviour's command, to make disciples of all nations. If this mission goes forward as it has been thus auspiciously commenced, we may confidently look for great and glorious results. A good beginning has been made. A foothold has been secured. Gospel seed has been sown. It is already springing up. "Say not ye, there are four months, and then cometh harvest? Behold, I say unto you, lift up your eyes, and look on the fields, for they are white already to harvest."—John iv: 35.

XIX.

AN AMERICAN MISSIONARY WITH HIS COAT OFF, AND AN HAWAIIAN MISSIONARY WITH HIS SLEEVES ROLLED UP.

We witnessed a scene on one of the islets encircling the lagoon of Ebon, which would have gratified the friends of education and missions. After the Sabbath morning services at the Mission Station, it was our privilege to accompany Messrs. Doane and Aea to their out-station on the opposite side of the lagoon. We were just one hour crossing the lagoon. On approaching the shore, Mr. Doane skilfully piloted our boat through a narrow opening in the reef, scarcely wide enough to allow the boat to pass. We entered the smooth waters within the barrier reef, and skimming along over beds of coral, of every shape, variety and color, saw the fish darting in and out from under the rocky branching marine forest.

As we landed, a group of bright-eyed and laughing children gave us a cordial welcome. We proceeded immediately to the meeting or school house, where an audience of over one hundred soon gathered. The females were all modestly attired, their hair neatly combed and parted, and many wore chaplets of fresh flowers. The house was filled, even overflowing, and as closely packed as the hold of a slaver. The Rev. Mr. Doane conducted the services. He introduced the strangers, who made short addresses. Then followed the school exercise. The whole audience, old and young, arranged themselves into groups of about eight or ten. Mr. Doane, Aea, and a few young men, or rather boys, who could read, sat down upon the mats to teach these ignorant islanders the rudiments of their language. Truly the scene was one to be remembered by those of us to whom such scenes were new. *Mr. Doane took of his coat, and Aea rolled up his sleeves.* They engaged in the work with an energy and zeal, earnestness and cheerfulness, that imparted life and animation to the school, which banished everything like drowsiness or inattention. Every eye and ear was awake. We never saw more hearty study or more promising pupils. The sounds of

" ba, be, bo, bu,

am, om, im, um, em,"

are still ringing in our ears. The voices of the Ebonites are by no means harsh or unpleasant. Mr. Doane has arranged some of the elementary exercises, in such a manner that they form a simple chant, rendering the lessons very easy of remembrance. The interesting school was opened by singing "There is a Happy Land," and closed by a hymn, in the Ebon language.

XX.

DEFERENCE TO RANK AMONG MARSHALL ISLANDERS.

"Honor thy Father and thy Mother,"

Is a command which God gave to Moses upon Sinai. The Marshall Islanders reverse this law, and inculcate the principle, "parents honor your children." The oldest son of a family rules the household. He is never checked or restrained, but his will is law and his caprice the rule. While visiting Mr. Doane's family, we noticed a chief pass some food to his little son, which had been given him by Mr. Doane. The father did not even taste of the food, before offering it to his son. We were informed that should the oldest son even kill his father, or any member of the family, he would not be called to account!

One of the most serious difficulties into which Mr. Doane has ever been brought, was when he unintentionally treated the oldest son of a high chief, in a manner which was interpreted as an insult by the chief. The lad insulted was a young *sans culotte* sprig of the highest blood. His father fired up and threatened. He defied the terrors of a man-of-war! He intimated that the missionary's life might be the forfeiture, or that he might be *disposed of* as so many other foreigners had been! Mr. Doane calmly remonstrated. The chief then intimated that a present would appease his wrath and restore the insulted honor of his son. " No," said the missionary, "I came here to teach you, not to make you presents." He then pointed out to him the law of God, and read the ten commandments, closing the interview with prayer, as described in another part of the sketches.

Jealousy respecting rank is not confined to rulers and princes of enlightened and civilized nations. We have never known stronger feelings manifested among any people upon this subject, than among the naked savages of the Marshall Islands. A line marked and distinct is drawn between chiefs and common people. There is no crossing that with impunity. We asked the Rev. Mr. Doane, what crimes were punishable? He replied, "none but insult to chiefs." The death penalty is not unfrequently inflicted for this crime. Only a few days before our arrival at Ebon, a young man was put to death, on the merest suspicion, and after his death it was ascertained that he was innocent.

While the chiefs are so very jealous upon this subject, still they mingle among their people, and outwardly but slight deference is paid to the chiefs.

Among the chiefs, everything, in regard to rank, depends upon who was a chief's mother. The female gives rank. Their ideas and laws respecting marriage are very peculiar. A chief of the first class must marry a woman of the second class, and their children will be second class chiefs. A first class woman must marry a second class chief, and their children will belong to the first class. These rules are rigidly enforced. Polygamy exists among them. Some have as many as four or five wives, although we heard of none who carried their ideas o polygamy to the extent of Brigham Young and his followers.

XXI.

FAREWELL GLANCE AT MARSHALL ISLANDS.

These islands are thirty in number. Fifteen forming the Ralick or Western Chain, and fifteen forming the Radack or Eastern Chain. The population is estimated at 10,000; the Ralickers numbering 6,000, and the Radackers, 4,000. Each chain of islands has its own chiefs, and are independent of each other, although the chiefs of the Ralick Chain entertain the idea of *nominal* supremacy. There was a rumor, at the time of our visit, that the chiefs of the Ralick Chain were about to assert and endeavor to maintain their authority over their less powerful neighbors.

The food of the natives consists of bread fruit, jack fruit, (a species of bread fruit,) cocoa nuts, pandanus fruit, and fish. The manufacture of cocoanut oil has been commenced at Ebon, Messrs. Stapenhorst and Hoffschlaeger of Honolulu, having recently purchased land and erected the necessary buildings. It was estimated that nearly one hundred barrels of oil would be collected this year. As yet tobacco is the principal article of barter for oil.

All the islands of both chains are coral, low and lagoon shaped. There is more verdure upon these than upon the Gilbert Islands. They are situated in a region of the Pacific where the trade winds blow very strong and are accompanied by heavy thunder and lightning. They range from 4 ° to 12 ° N. L., and 165 ° to 172 ° E. L. The two chains of islands run nearly N. W. and S. E., and are parallel to each other. The whole group takes its name of *Marshall Islands*, from Capt. Marshall, of the English Navy, who visited them in the year 1788, commanding the *Scarborough*. The visits of the celebrated Russian Navigator, Kotzebue, to the Radack Chain, are full of interest as described in his voyages, published in London, 1821, in three volumes. These islands, however, have never been thoroughly explored, and are very incorrectly laid down upon the charts. The notices which have been published respecting them in Colton's large Atlas, or any other geographical works, are exceedingly meagre, incorrect, and unsatisfactory. Dr. Gulick's lecture upon the Marshall Islands, is higly interesting and instructive.

We now take our leave of the Marshall Islands and their inhabitants. Our visit opened up to view, a new phase of Polynesian life. We there saw the humble and devoted missionaries laboriously engaged in the work of reducing the language to a written form, teaching school and preaching to the people. After having enjoyed their hospitality and Christian fellowship, we took our departure, bringing away Mrs. Doane and her two little children, who left on account of her own health and the sickness of the youngest child. Never shall we forget that parting scene. This hymn was sung:

> " How vain is all beneath the skies !
> How transient every earthly bliss !
> How slender all the fondest ties,
> That bind us to a world like this, &c., &c.

*   *   *   *   *

> Then let the hope of joys to come,
> Dispel our cares, and chase our fears ;
> If God be ours, we're travelling home,
> Though passing through a vale of tears."

The Rev. Mr. Doane offered a prayer in the Ebon language, and it was followed by a prayer in English. We saw a number of the native Christians, or "lovers of Jesus," pass around to the state-room window and bid Mrs. Doane farewell, with many tears. It would have subdued the stoutest soul, to have witnessed the missionary part with his wife and children, and then step into his boat and steer for his lonely home ! There may be a romance about the missionary life, when viewed from the shores of Christian England and America, but all romance is dissipated and it puts on a stern reality when the real experience comes. As we stood upon the quarter deck of the *Morning Star*, conversing with the Rev. Mr. Doane, and taking a last look at the shores of Ebon, we said, " It is hard for you to part with your family, and go there to labor alone." His only reply was, " I could not, if I did not feel that Jesus was my companion." Surely it was no unmeaning language of our Saviour, " Lo, I am with you alway, even unto the end of the world." While this scene was passing, the sailors were heaving at the anchor, and the sails were loosening. We were soon off and bound for Strong's Island, but with the glass, we watched that little boat, rising and falling with the swell, until it was lost in the distance. When that happy family will be again united, is known only to the Master, in whose cause they labor.

XXII.

UALAN, STRONG'S ISLAND, OR KUSAIE.

In reading books upon Polynesia, and examining charts of the Pacific, there is nothing more perplexing than the variety of names applied to the same islands, or group. Ualan, Strong's Island or Kusaie, is a good illustration of this remark. We will now explain the several terms or names applied to this island.

UALAN, is the usual name found upon charts, and upon large atlases. This is the name which the natives apply to the large or main island, while *Lila*, is that of the small island.

STRONG'S ISLAND.—This is the name usually applied to the island, by whalers and seafaring people. It was given to the island by Capt. Crozer, commanding an American ship, who was the discoverer in 1804.

KUSAIE.—This is the name, by which the missionaries prefer to call the island. It is really the most appropriate name, as the native term to be applied to the two islands, viz : of Ualan and Lila.

The principal island, Ualan, is twenty-four miles in circumference, and the small island, Lila, about two miles. In ancient times, the large island was conquered by the inhabitants of the small island, and to the present time, remains tributary. The King resides upon the small island. The mission premises are also located upon it. It is separated, from the large, by a narrow channel of the eighth of a mile in width. Both are densely wooded, with cocoanut, breadfruit, mangrove and numerous other tropical trees. The forests are a perfect jungle. The large island is formed of two mountains towering to the height of about 2,000 feet, which may be seen a long distance at sea. The forests are intersected by numerous small streams. The climate is very humid, as we can testify! Strong winds prevail. Frequently the rains are accompanied by heavy thunder and vivid flashes of lightning. There are three harbors upon the island.

XXIII.

RUINS ON KUSAIE.

Very conflicting statements have been published respecting the ruins on Kusaie. We almost expected to behold the ruins of

" The cloud capp'd towers, the gorgeous palaces,"

covered with mosses and ivy, while from other reports, we were not led to expect any thing remarkable.

We found this to be the simple truth. The small Island of Lila, is surrounded by a wall, five or six feet high, but now very much dilapidated. The island is intersected and cut up by walls running in various directions, enclosing areas varying from a few to many acres. Some portions of these walls, are very massive, varying from five to twenty-five feet in height and proportionately broad or thick. The stones composing the walls were gathered from the island but a part were brought a long distance from the main island. This is true of some very large pentagonal basaltic rocks. Some of these rocks are very large. We saw specimens, which it would require half of the present inhabitants of the island to move and elevate to their present position.

We copy the following sentences from Dr. Gulick's third lecture:

" From M. D'Urville's reports and from the accounts of sea captains we had received glowing ideas of the architectural exhibitions on Lila; we were to find a native city handsomely laid out, with paved streets, and at frequent intervals handsome piles of stone-cut masonry. On the contrary, we found nothing but muddy paths, zigzagging hither and thither over rubbish and stones. There were many stone walls three or four feet high, evidently of very recent origin; and scattered among the groves were indeed evidences of ancient labor, consisting of artificial islets, built up above high tide level, and almost cyclopian lines and enclosures of stone walls. Banyan like trees had in many cases sent their roots into the very center of these structures, and from some spots the stones have been entirely removed. A line of stone, varying in height in different parts, surrounds a considerable portion of the central hill of Lila. Not far from the King's and his eldest son's residences are several enclosures about two hundred by one hundred feet, with walls twenty feet high, and in some places at the foundations twelve feet thick. We partially traced at least one very much larger but less perfect enclosure. The walls are built of basaltic stones, occasionally filled in with coral. Some of the rocks are very large irregular masses, while others are beautiful pentagonal prisms. There is not the remotest trace upon any of them of a stone-cutter's adze. Along the south western shore are a number of canals communicating with the harbor and in which the sea ebbs and flows. The sides of the canals are in some cases crumbled, but bear evident tokens of having been artificially built; and the islets themselves are evidently in a considerable degree artificial, composed principally of coral stones, the rubbels of the canals themselves. These canals intersected each other, and so formed islets, on at least one of which is found a towering stone enclosure. Mangrove trees have in many cases choked up these watery courses, and with other kinds of trees on the islets have nearly buried the whole in a shade most congenial with the thoughts excited by these relics of a dimmer age than that which we might hope had now dawned upon them.

"King George afterward informed us that these walls were built by the former inhabitants. Many of the larger rocks were brought from the main island on rafts. When we asked how such heavy blocks could be elevated so high, he replied they were rolled up from one level to another on inclined planes of logs and stones. As to their uses, he said the wall about the hill was for defense from aggressors from the main island, and that many of the remaining walls were in honor of the dead. Nothing could be more improbable or unsatisfactory than to import a company of buccaneers, or any civilized people, to build what could not be at all to their purpose, nor to the credit of their architectural talents; and what it would have been morally impossible for them to have done. The inhabitants of Kusaie are even now skilled in wall building. We were told that one of their most decisive evidences of public grief is to rebuild the wall about the premises of a bereaved chief; and to this day the chiefs are buried in one of the ancient enclosures, as though they were the mausoleums of the great. Possibly they may in the first instance have been built about royal residences, and on the decease of the builders have become their magnificent sepulchres, though the analogy of present Micronesian customs decides against it."

XXIV.

WEATHER BOUND ON KUSAIE.

It is related of a voyager in the South Pacific, that he once visited an island inhabited by savages, where a white man was not safe. During a subsequent voyage the ship in which he sailed, was wrecked upon the same island. He confidently expected that an untimely end would be his certain fate. Soon however he was met by a friendly native, who kindly pointed the wrecked man to the house of the "Mikinari." Hope now succeeded to fear in the sailor's mind. He exclaimed, "All's well, there is a missionary here."

We have never been wrecked, but we have been weather-bound, and unable to join our vessel. We landed on Kusaie, early Sabbath morning, and were unable to communicate with the *Morning Star*, until the following Friday. Not only did we enjoy the feeling of security among Kusaiens, but we also enjoyed the kind entertainment of a most hospitable family. We shall not very soon forget the kindness and generous treatment we experieuced from Mr. and Mrs. Snow, the only white persons residing upon the island. During the period of our detention, we enjoyed an excellent opportunity for picking up numerous items of historical and local interest, visiting the dwellings of the inhabitants, observing their habits and customs, besides examining the progress of the people in their appreciation of the missionary's efforts to raise them in the scale of civilization, and impart to them the invaluable blessings of Christianity. The Sabbath being our first day spent among the Kusaiens, naturally leads us to refer, in the first place, to Kusaie as a mission field.

XXV.

MISSION ON KUSAIE.

This mission was established in the autumn of 1852, by the Rev. B. G. Snow and wife. They were left there by the schooner *Caroline*, commanded by Capt. Holdsworth, during the successful trip of that vessel to Micronesia, on a missionary enterprise. The missionaries were welcomed by King George, who not only allowed them a residence, but gave them a most cordial welcome, and who proved to the day of his death, (September 9th, 1854,) a firm and steadfast friend of the missionary. Before his death he offered the most gratifying evidence that his soul had embraced the glorious doctrines of Christianity, as unfolded and explained by Mr. Snow. The King's death threw a dark shadow over the prospects of the mission, for his successor was a man possessed of the very opposite traits of character, who died in about two years, as he lived, the debased slave of lust and drunkenness. He was succeeded by the present chief ruler, whose conduct and policy towards the mission, is by no means one of opposition, but rather that of indifference. He uniformly treats the missionary with kindness, and is a friendly neighbor, comes to meeting upon the Sabbath morning, and like too many in Christian lands, during the week is a faithful servant of this world.

The King was almost the first Kusaien to whom we were introduced, for we found him at church before the audience had assembled. Soon after we entered, an audience gathered of about one hundred. The men were seated cross-legged upon mats, in the rear. The King and three high chiefs upon benches, and the females and children in front of the missionary, while the missionary's family and strangers were disposed of on the left of the desk.

A manuscript collection of hymns, was handed us, and others received the same, for a Kusaien had never as yet looked upon a printed page of his language, although this gratification was soon afforded him, as the *Morning Star* brought 300 copies of a small primer and hymn book printed in the Kusaien language. Mr. Snow gave out the hymns, and conducted the services, after the usual method in our congregations, excepting that he called upon the strangers for some remarks, which he interpreted. The audience was respectful and attentive. The utmost decorum prevailed during the exercises. The closing hymn, was the translation of that familiar English Hymn,

> "The Saviour calls—let every one
> Attend the heavenly sound ;
> Ye doubting souls ! dismiss your fear,
> Hope smiles reviving round."

We very much doubt whether Mrs. Steele, the author of this hymn, the friend of Addison, imagined it would ever be translated into the language of a savage tribe upon an island of the Pacific, not to be discovered until after she had been dead for a hundred years.

After the morning exercises were closed, the Sabbath School convened, when about twenty-five remained. Through Mr. Snow as interpreter, the strangers present endeavored to interest the pupils.

At the afternoon service, gathered, what Mr. Snow denominates " his Christian congregation." Among them appeared Kedukka and family, who have for some years professed a strong attachment to the gospel. Several others are affording the gratifying evidence of having been born again, and stand as candidates for church membership, while others show an inquiring state of mind. Kedukka, mentioned above, evinces a strong determination to make his light shine. He has commenced itinerating through the villages upon the island, and appears to make known among his benighted fellow islanders, the truths of the gospel.

On the following Wednesday afternoon, a most interesting prayer-meeting was held at the house of the missionaries, when native Christians and strangers from abroad, " felt it good to be there." There was distributed for the first time, copies of *printed* hymns.

While the labors of Mr. and Mrs. Snow were peculiarly designed for the natives of Kusaie, we feel that they have also accomplished a most important work in behalf of seamen. Oftentimes during their residence there, the harbors of the island have been visited by numerous whale ships, sometimes fifteen or twenty at a time ; but we shall refer to this topic under another heading.

In addition to Mr. Snow's labors at the station, he is accustomed to make tours about the island—preaching from village to village. These are very laborious. The whole south side of the large island seems much inclined to receive missionary labors, while the northern part is opposed, and holds on to its former superstitions. The work however has begun and will spread, and unquestionably should the mission be prosecuted, the entire population will be soon brought under Christian influences.

As we shall show in another paper, the inhabitants of Kusaie are rapidly diminishing in numbers. This fact in connection with the urgent call for missionary labor at the Marshall Islands, has led to the prospective removal of Mr. and Mrs. Snow to Ebon, when the *Morning Star* shall make another trip to Micronesia. His removal has been decided upon by his associates of the mission, and approved of by the Prudential Committee of the American Board of Foreign Missions at Boston. It is now contemplated to supply his place by an Hawaiian issionary, as soon as necessary arrangements can be made.

XXVI.

GOVERNMENT AND CUSTOMS OF KUSAIENS.

We have learned some interesting facts about this people. They have the most exact system of clannish tribal relationships that could well be conceived of. The name for tribe is *Seuf*.

There are *four* tribes, no more nor less from time immemorial. The names of the tribes and their order, are as follows :

Peinuii, Tou, Lisuge, and *Neus*.

Peinuii, means true or correct.

Tou, is the name of a sacred eel.

Lisuge, a partition.

Neus, is the name for foot.

The Kusaiens marry in the most indiscriminate manner possible. From time immemorial the children follow the mother. The Jews were never more exact in their lineage than this people are in preserving their line of descent.

PRINCIPAL CHIEF.—This office is not hereditary. Though not quite elective among the near relatives of the deceased sachem of the same tribe, yet in the prospective demise of the Togusa or King, there is a good deal of what American politicians would call log-rolling, for the King-ship, and after all is done, the chief of another tribe may succeed to the throne, if the *popular feeling* among the people sets strongly in that direction.

A son of a former *Togusa* or King, may succeed to his father; so also the son of a brother, or a sister, of the *Togusa,* although there is no law in regard to such a course.

So far as Mr. Snow has been able to learn from observation or inquiry, the duties of the Togusa are not confined to affairs of peace. In a war which the natives had with some foreigners in '57, who endeavored to get possession of the island, the Togusa, was commander-in-chief of the tribes. Nothing could be done without his permission or direction. When peace was made by the arrival of the *Morning Star,* the Togusa was the sole executive in the crisis, though there was previously held a convention for consultation among all the chiefs.

We learned from Mr. Snow the following interesting facts respecting the bonds of relationship. If a man has a dozen brothers, his children have as many fathers, besides their natural father, and all the children of those mothers are brothers and sisters. All the fathers, sisters or mothers to his children, and the sister's children, are brothers and sisters to her brother's children. The same law holds good on the mother's side.

The names of individuals are not changed from the cradle to the grave, unless the person is exalted to become a chief. Then the common name is dropped and *he or she* goes by the official name. Every male chiefish title, has a corresponding female chiefish title, viz :

Togusa male title, *Kosa* female title. Should the chief have several wives, but one can bear the official title. When the husband dies, the female title is gradually dropped. If another immediately succeeds to the chieftain-ship, the title is dropped at once, and all the honors, titles, lands, servants &c., succeed to the chief elect.

Mr. Snow relates the following facts in regard to the absolute subserviency of the people to their chiefs or their king, *e. g.*: the male child of the daughter of old King George—this daughter being the wife of the second chief in authority—receives from her mother the same deferential regard that he would if he were a chief already titled. In addressing the child, though but an infant, the prefix *Se*, equivalent to our *Sir* or *Honorable*, is invariably employed. This brother must never touch the child's head, although he may handle other parts of the child's body, oil or wash it, but no greater offense could be given to the parents of the child than for him to touch any part of the body above the shoulders. Now if this daughter of the old king had an older sister, then this one of whom we have been speaking, would be obliged to exhibit the same tokens of respect to the older sister's child or children. All these ceremonies going or tending to keep the idea of the superiority of the mother, that the honors and royalty are lodged in her hereditarily.

Mr. Snow furnished me with the following interesting facts in regard to their tribal laws, relating to help in sickness. If one is sick or in distress, or needs help in any other way, then it is the duty of the tribe to which he belongs to render that help. They, as speedily as possible, gather about those in distress, and remain with them until relieved, or removed by death. If removed by death, they continue their attentions, supplying all the necessaries for four days of feasting after death. This is a law of the tribes, and it altereth not.

Mr. S. stated the following custom among them, in regard to the treatment of a chief's child, until it can crawl. It must never lie upon the floor, but be held, night and day, month after month in the arms of nurses and servants. The person holding the child, must allow its neck to rest upon the arm, that when the child is at rest, the head falls back.

XXVII.

DECREASE OF POPULATION ON KUSAIE.

January 5, 1858, the Rev. Mr. Snow thus wrote to the editors of the *Missionary Herald*, as appears from the April No. of the *Herald*, for 1859. "I have just finished taking the census of the island again, and find that there are now about 830 inhabitants—518 males and 312 females, including children; making the proportion of males to females about 5 to 3. When I took the census about two and a half years ago, the population was a few over 1100. This shows that our people are diminishing at a rapid rate, but the war has had some hand in the diminution the past year. I have found more infants upon the island than at any other time when I have taken the census. * * *. When the books are opened there will be a scene presented from these islands of the Pacific where ships have been accustomed to touch, at which so called civilization will hang her head, and call upon the mountains and rocks to fall upon her, and if possible hide her shame from the gaze of the assembled universe. For at the bar of God, these men from Christian lands will find there is such a thing as shame and remorse."

At our visit, Mr. Snow allowed us to copy the following memoranda from his Journal: "Dec. 29, 1860. Finished taking the census to-day. I make 748 in all—523 in Ualan and 225 in Lila. The males of the adults and older children 411, while the females of the same were 258. But of the younger children and infants the males were 37 and females 42, thus making the proportion of the older of the women to the men 0.63, while with the children, it is 1.13. This certaininly is a hopeful phase for the restoration of the race, and I desire to thank God that it is so."

XXVIII.

MISSIONARY OFFICIATING AS SEAMEN'S CHAPLAIN.

The Rev. G. B. Snow, at Strong's Island or Kusaie, has been accustomed to officiate as Chaplain, when seamen were in port. In former years many English and American whale ships have visited that island for supplies. The bark *Superior*, Capt. R. D. Woods, visited Strong's Island in 1860, and sailed from thence to the Solomon's Islands, where the master and nearly all the crew were cruelly massacred by the natives. An account of their massacre has been extensively published in the island and American newspapers. The disaster took place in Sept. 1860. Capt. Hugh Mair, master of the English schooner, *Ariel*, thus writes from Rubiana, Solomon Islands, Nov. 30, 1860:

"On Sunday, the 16th, nine of the crew went ashore. The carpenter and two men went to the settlement and were murdered in one of the native huts. The natives then proceeded, in canoes and overland, to the ship; and those who came by land fell in with the remaining six, close to the beach, and murdered them. About 150 natives got on board the vessel, and made a rush on the crew, who were all on deck—except four who were in bed. Those on deck were immediately tomahawked, only two escaping by jumping down the main hatchway, and joining the four below in the forecastle. One of the crew, whom I recovered, saw the captain and second mate murdered by a native called 'Billy,' who has been to Sydney, and speaks English well. The chief Copan was the principal in this dreadful massacre. The six men below, being armed with lances, kept the natives from coming down the forecastle, until at last 'Billy' told my informant that if they came up they should not be hurt. At length, therefore, they did so, and were at once surrounded by the chief Copan's orders to be put to death. The chief America offered to buy three of the men, and he persuaded Copan to keep the other three to till the ground. These three, as I have already intimated, I could not recover."

While the *Superior* lay at Strong's Island, the Master, Capt. Wood, and his crew were accustomed to attend the native service upon the Sabbath. The news of the massacre was taken to the island by the *Morning Star.* The Rev. Mr. Snow and wife were deeply affected by the sad intelligence. Mr. Snow then exhibited the following extract from a letter which he had addressed the owners of the *Superior* in New Bedford. This letter was written and forwarded long before the news of the massacre was known. It was the *postscript* to a letter upon business, relating to a wreck, which had occurred at the island.

" P. S. Gentleman, allow me to detain you for a moment by expressing my interest in and high regard for this R. D. Wood. He has made our little island quite a port of entry since we have been located here, and from the first we have always hailed his coming with much pleasure. Among the almost entire licentious delinquencies of those who visit us, it affords me the truest pleasure to bear honorable testimony in favor of the uniformly pure and upright conduct of this Capt. Wood. Besides this, he has endeared himself to us by many an act of generous kindness in supplying some of our wants, and especially in bringing us some of our mails. Though not the most talkative of men, yet his occasional visits to our family in our isolated, but pleasant and happy home, have always been most welcome and afforded us much enjoyment. It may afford his good lady, some of his cousins and that favorite niece, some pleasure to hear thus of him, though it be from a stranger. Though we have seen less of Capt. Morrison of the *Daniel Wood,* yet it affords me sincere pleasure to bear equally high and honorable testimony concerning him. He has done us great kindness not only in our mail department, but also in bringing supplies from Honolulu."

On the last Sabbath the *Superior* lay at Strong's Island, the Rev. Mr. Snow preached the following discourse to the ship's company. Considering the untimely fate of so many interesting young men, far away from home and country, it may be interesting to their friends to learn that they should have conducted with so much propriety, during their last visit at a port where they could listen to the preaching of the gospel. This discourse was prepared without the most distant thought that it would ever be solicited for publication :

" And straightway Jesus constrained his disciples to get into a ship, and to go before him unto the other side.—MATHEW XIV:22.

There cluster about our text some of the most instructive incidents and transactions in the life of the Divine Redeemer. He had been spending a short season in his own city, Nazareth, trying to impart heavenly wisdom unto the friends of his earlier days. But it was soon seen that a prophet had no honor in his own country, nor even in his own house. Like many other foolish people, they loved things better that were " far fetched and dear bought." They were not to be instructed by the " Carpenter's son," not they. So " He did not many mighty works there because of their unbelief."   *   *   *

But let us turn our attention now to his disciples and that night upon the sea. While the Master was praying upon the mountains, the disciples were sailing on the waters. The disciples doubtless had a place in that prayer, and the chosen twelve thought and talked of their absent Lord. Four of those sailors at least, Simon Peter and Andrew his brother with the two sons of Zebedee were no strangers upon that lake. Many a long night had they sat in their boats alternately watching their nets and the Stars. They had thought of the sweet influences of the Pleiades, and the bands of Orion, they knew the hand that guided Arcturus and his sons. But now they had left their fishing tackle and their fathers and had been called to be fishers of men. The words and wonders of the preceeding day with the strangely abundant supper for that great multitude might have justly awakened their pride and feelings of admiration for their new master. But they are hardly out upon the sea ere they are beset with difficulties. A contrary wind and a boisterous sea kept them toiling in rowing for the livelong night; and they had hardly made half their passage, when the dawning day brought to their astonished vision what they had supposed to have been a spirit, and they cried out for fear. The apparition came up and made as though it would have passed. But Jesus seeing and hearing their fears immediately talked with them, and said in his well known voice, " Be of good cheer, it is I, be not afraid." His word to their spirits was like " Peace be still " to the troubled waters. As soon as he is recognized the impulsive Peter must try a walk upon the waters. "And Peter answered him and said, Lord, if it be thou, bid me come unto thee on the water." And he said, Come ! I suspect the "if it be thou," in his prayer shows that the thoughts of the ghost had not all been displaced for complete faith in his Master. For when he saw the wind boisterous he was afraid, and beginning to sink he cried for help. Immediately Jesus stretched forth his hand and caught him. Then the rebuke, " O thou of little faith, wherefore didst thou doubt?" The wet Peter and the welcome Jesus were soon in the ship, when the wind ceased. They soon had prayers, and it was a pleasant morning worship. For it is written, " Then they that were in the ship came and worshiped him, saying of a truth, thou art the Son of God." They were sore amazed in themselves, beyond measure, because they had forgotten the five loaves and the 5000. But ere they had finished their astonishment their passage is made, and they are all safely on shore with the opening duties of a new day before them. I hardly need pursue the narrative farther, though the following day is filled with incidents of peculiar and striking interest. We shall do better to pause here and gather a few practical lessons from what we have already witnessed. My audience will not object to our gathering some lessons from this night on the sea.

I. *Those who enter the service of Christ need not abandon the sea.*

I should almost feel like begging pardon of my seafaring friends for making such a remark, had not the assertion been so often made to me by those first in authority, that it is no use to try to be religious till we are done with whaling, and have quit the sea. I am aware that such remarks may be made to parry off the truth and to quiet an uneasy conscience, rather than as an honest expression of an intelligent man. And yet, my hearers, will bear me witness that giving utterance to such a sentiment whenever the claims of God and the duties of religion are urged upon the conscience, would soon make a sentiment, however false, an absolute fact in its practical influence upon the lives of men. But God allows no such let off. His claims upon the love and service of his intelligent creatures are not limited to the land ; they extend from sea to sea, and from the river to the ends of the earth. And my heart rises in thankfulness to God that this is not mere theory. The witnesses upon the sea, though not so many as we could desire, have yet been very numerous, and sometimes of very marked and distinguishing clearness, from that old voyager in the ark to the present time. Thanks be to God that he has always had a seed to serve him on the sea. And perhaps at no period in the past has the number of these been more rapidly multiplying than within a year or two of the present time. The means too are constantly multiplying to effect this same end. The intelligent sympathies also of the Christian world, are being more and more wisely awakened and turned to the great and glorious result of gathering the fullness of the sea into the Kingdom of God. My friends of the *Superior* can you not trace growing emotions in your own hearts which will bear favorable testimony to the truth of these remarks ? If so, yield your hearts to those emotions and you will soon find in your own happy experience that those who enter the service of christ need not abandon the sea.

II. Another lesson from that night upon the sea is *that it is always safe to obey Christ.*

It is true that they had not the bodily presence of their Divine Master on board, as at another time when crossing the lake of Genesaret, he was asleep in the hinder part of the ship, but they had what was just as good for their safety, his command, "Get into the ship and go unto the other side." There was nothing in the articles about Peter leaving the ship and trying to foot it. And he seemed to have gained only a wetting for his folly and a reprimand for his rashness. Had John tried it, I suspect he could have gone much more safely than did Peter. But he had the wisdom to serve his Master where his Master put him. Peter would have done much better to have kept his seat at the oar. Deserters, even when it is done under the cloak of piety, are only losers in the end. How many have read about Peter's folly since that night ! and how much talk there has been about it! We are apt to remember and talk of the foolish things that men do, much longer than we do their wise things. The disciples had a head wind and a rough sea, so that they were all night in making a passage which might have been made in two hours. So that being a servant of Christ, don't exempt from trials even at sea. But how often contrary winds occasion hard thoughts of God, and hard words, too, sometimes ! Had the disciples made a quick passage, they and the world had probably never known that illustration of Divine power in the Saviour, his walking upon the water. Be sure that you have an ear and a heart intent upon hearing and obeying the commands of Christ, and you need have no fears concerning the winds or the waves. Every event will have its lessons of wisdom to teach, and each trial of faith and patience will bring good to the heart, though there may be less gold in the pocket. Safety and welfare of the ship is much more thought of and planned for than the safety and welfare of the soul. Good for the voyage, is oftener the question than "will it be good for heaven!" While if a thing is good for heaven, it certainly can't be bad for a voyage. There are no tests of friendship where there are no trials.

The being *wind* bound is one thing, the being *will* bound is quite another. The one may keep from going to sea for awhile, the other may keep from going to heaven forever. For the words of Christ are "Ye *will* not come unto me, that ye might have life." There was an old Governor of Israel, Joshua by name, who said "*as for me and my house, we will serve the Lord.*" I knew another of less note, but equally wise in that thing, and he was a sailor. When urged to the surrender of his will to God, exclaimed, "I will serve God or nobody." By so doing they are both safe for heaven. You who hear me now, "Go and do likewise," and you will be equally safe for the same place.

III. A third point of instruction is, *that sailors should never forget the Saviour.*

No class of people in all the world were so honored as sailors in the choice which Christ made of his disciples. One-third of the whole number were chosen from that class alone. Then to carry the honor still further, he chose his three favorite disciples out of those four. Has this distinction been well repaid in the gratitude and love of seamen? Your better acquaintance with seamen than mine, better qualifies you to answer the question. Let me put the question more practically: Do you, yourselves acknowledge your indebtedness to Christ on this account? Perhaps it has not been sufficiently thought of to be intelligently answered. It certainly calls loudly for your consideration. "For unto whomsoever much is given, of him shall be much required." Be assured my friends, Christ has strong claims upon seamen. And I ask you as men belonging to that class, have not those claims been sufficiently long protested? Is it not time that you yourselves acknowledged those claims and were paying your dues? From our stand point it would seem that the Saviour was not wise in having so many seamen with him as his intimate friends and counsellors. For though they come from almost every land, it is a pity that more don't find their way back again; but the pity is still greater, that of those who do return, so few have been improved during their absence. So fearful is the state of things in this regard, that I have seldom found an observing or sensible seaman who would choose a sailor's life for his own boy. And in all my intercourse with the world, I have never found a class of men, as a class, among whom there are so few christians. But notwithstanding these drawbacks, I am far from attributing want of wisdom and the broadest forecast to the course pursued by our blessed Saviour. The very fact that sailors come from all lands and go to all lands is a matter of great interest in this connection. Get the genuine leaven of Christianity into this mass, and there is a mighty working power. It is felt at home and abroad, on sea and on shore. The lowest and most despised has his circle of interests and of influences. Sanctify it and he becomes powerful. How much more so would it be when those interests and influences were backed up by intelligence and by official standing. These wide and powerful influences are not always to be lost to the church. The sailor will ere long acknowledge the claims of the Saviour, he will hear and heed the call, "Follow me and I will make you fishers of men." And the sacrifice will not be so great to them as to many of us landsmen, to respond to that dying command of the great Redeemer, "Go ye into all the world and preach the Gospel to every creature." For he goes there already without the commission. How much more will he go there when his heart becomes fired with the love of christ, and he sees in the Jesus of Nazareth the dearest of friends and the Saviour of his own immortal soul. His heart will become an altar of incense, and his life, a perpetual thank-offering.

IV. If you want to make a safe passage and reach a good port at last, *take Christ with you.*

I hardly need say more under this head than to assure you that without taking Christ, there is no possibility of such a result. "For there is none other name under heaven given among men whereby we must be saved." That name is Jesus Christ,

> " Dearest of all names above,
> My Jesus and my God !
> Who can resist thy heavenly love,
> Or trifle with thy blood ?"

You are aware that it is a law of nations that no ship shall enter port with contraband freight on board. Before she can enter, that freight must be moved, or there is a liability to capture and condemnation. All sin is contraband at the port of heaven, and there is no possibility of escaping detection. If you were sure of a chance to stop somewhere and make a change, it might be safe though not very wise to continue your present course. But there is no such insurance company established. A great many have tried it and failed. There is no capital to start with, so all their policies have been found useless. It is well to know this at the outset.

But God has sent an agent, and established a house to attend to all such business. That agent is the one I am now recommending to your consideration. He will take all your contraband articles off your hands and give you the best marketable freight. And what is very singular, he charges nothing for his commission.

There is one very simple and very reasonable condition in the policy, which must be affectionately subscribed to before he will sign the papers that will insure your safe entrance into the port of heaven. I hardly need tell you that that condition is perfect loyalty to the Great Sovereign. Give an assurance of this and you will get free papers, a sure passport, wonderful to say, signed with the blood of the agent. Having this, your voyage may be shorter or longer, perilous or otherwise, nothing will ever really harm you; blow high or blow low, storm or sunshine, head winds or fair winds or no winds at all, it will be all the same at last, provided you preserve with the strictest fidelity your loyalty. In the book of principles which the great Sovereign has given to teach us how to be loyal, there is something very encouraging given to show that those who are beset with great trials and peculiar difficulties are treated with marked consideration by the Great Sovereign himself. Let me read it to you from the Book. Rev. vii:13—17.

> Then haste, O Sailor! to be wise,
> Stay not for the morrow's sun ;
> Wisdom warns thee from the skies,
> All the paths of death to shun.

> Haste and mercy, now implore :
> Stay not for the morrow's sun,
> Thy probation may be o'er,
> Ere this evening's work is done.

> Haste, O Sailor! now return ;
> Stay not for the morrow's sun,
> Lest thy lamp should cease to burn
> Ere salvation's work is done.

> Haste while yet thou cans't be blest
> Stay not for the morrow's sun ;
> Death may thy poor soul arrest,
> Ere the morrow is begun.

XXIX.

ONE MAN CANNOT KNOW EVERYTHING, YET MAY KNOW SOME THINGS.

On the eve of our departure from Honolulu there was passed into our hands a short note, which we hastily deposited in our vest pocket, and did not discover it until our cruise was partly finished. It read after this manner :

" Mr. Damon will greatly oblige Dr. Hillebrand, if he will procure and press the leaves and grasses of the various localities, which he is about to visit in Micronesia."

Whether we have in the least obliged our friend by the specimens of plants and seeds, which we have gathered, is quite uncertain, for we must confess our ignorance of botany, *scientifically* speaking, although our eye can discern beauties in the ."lilies of the field." We take a sincere pleasure in observing works of nature, although we do not profess, with the votaries of the natural sciences, "to feast on raptures ever new," as they examine plants, shells, rocks, corals, fish, bugs, birds, animals, and the endless variety of genera and species which the God of nature has scattered so profusely over the islands, islets, reefs and rocks, throughout the teeming waters of Micronesia.

If we ever coveted the mental powers of an Humboldt, Agassiz,

Cuvier, Buffon, Lyell, Hitchcock, Dana, *Pease and Hillebrand*, it was when rambling over the coral reefs of Apaiang and Tarawa, or through the forests of Ebon and Kusaie, or canoe-sailing over the shoals and lagoons of Ponapi, or listening to the chattering bats of Kusaie, or the parrots of Ponapi. We saw fish, insects, grubs, slugs, and polypi with numberless tentacula, sufficient to have riveted the attention and enraptured the soul of a naturalist for weeks and years. The air, land and water teem with living creatures; then, too, upon those coral reefs, our mental vision was sufficiently acute to discern some of their mysterious wonders. How many millions of those busy reef-builders, we must have crushed at every step, for the researches of an Ehrenberg have established the fact that "nine millions of some of these animalcula may live in a space not larger than a mustard seed." (See Hitchcock's "Religious Truth illustrated from Science.") But natural science is not our province, we can assert however without fear of overstating the truth, that there are fields of natural history to be explored in Micronesia, which will amply reward the labors of the devotees of science for many years to come. Mr. Garrett spent weeks upon the reefs of Apaiang, and then left them as he asserted, but half explored, and doubtless ere this, Prof. Agassiz has exhibited Mr. Garrett's collections to the admiring classes of Cambridge University.

While visiting Tarawa, we endeavored most faithfully to procure a human skull, to enrich the collection of our phrenological and ethnological friend, Mr. Green, the Acting British Consul at Honolulu. We visited a very Golgotha, where the skulls lay upon the ground thick as leaves in the vale of Vallambrosa, but the King would not allow us to take one away. The Kingsmill Islanders highly prize the skulls of their deceased relatives. After death, they clean and oil them, and then carefully deposit them in their houses.

In our visits to the different islands and seeing the field of scientific research spread out before us, we felt how vastly important to be able to investigate the vegetable, animal and mineral kingdoms. A traveler, by sea or land, who would go forth fully prepared to improve every advantage and explore every object of interest, should be qualified, with the ability of the great Leibnitz, "to drive all the sciences abreast." Who but Humboldt could do this?

Although we were not able to devote much time to the collection of specimens of natural history during our brief sojourn at the various mission stations where we touched, yet we found our time more than occupied, day and night, in making inquiries respecting the genus *homo*, his habits, customs, practices, languages, institutions, and governments, believing with Pope, that the

"Proper study of mankind is man."

Man, as exhibited, and as he appeared at the four localities, at which we touched, presents a great diversity of physiological, psychological and *theological* points of interest.

This point was a special subject of inquiry with us. Do the heathen, or men living without the light of revealed religion, possess a knowledge of what is morally right and wrong? From our inquiries

7

among the debased and torpid Kingsmill Islanders, the sharp and keen Ebonites, the calm and obsequious Kusaiens, and the shrewd and feast-loving Ponapians, we answer most unhesitatingly, *man without a Divine Revelation is a morally accountable being,* agreeable to the language of the Apostle Paul, in the second chapter of his Epistle to the Romans, wherein he says, " For when the Gentiles, which have not the law, do by nature the things contained in the law, these having not the law, are a law unto themselves, *which show the work of the law written in their hearts, their conscience also bearing witness* and their thoughts the meanwhile accusing or else excusing one another." But it may be asked wherein does the conscience of the heathen bear witness to what is right and wrong? We answer, they know and *feel* that it is wrong to steal, to lie, to kill, to commit adultery. The heathen punish for such crimes, and oftentimes that punishment is most summary. The death-penalty quickly follows the perpetration of the crime. The Marshall Islanders, and the Kusaiens, even now live in dread of being called to account for the ships they have cut off and seamen they have murdered. Their consciences are by no means at rest. It is no easy matter to obtain information upon those subjects. We were informed upon the most reliable authority that the chiefs of those islands would probably punish with death those of their subjects, whom they discovered revealing facts relating to those massacres. At one time the Marshall Islanders, when a terrible storm was raging, *thought* they saw a fleet of men-of-war in the distant horizon, coming down upon their islands, to call them to account. Did not their consciences bear witness? This is a most interesting subject in its bearing upon the question of human responsibility, and we are inclined to protract our remarks to an undue length.

XXX.

KUSAIEN LANGUAGE.

The language of the inhabitants of Kusaie, exhibits some very singular linguistical features. Before the missionaries landed upon the island, the natives had acquired a smattering of the English language. This was merely the result of their intercourse with foreigners, principally with seamen. They were able to employ intelligently a greater number of English words than those Hawaiians who have lived for years in foreign families in Honolulu. So great was their knowledge of English, that Mr. Snow endeavored for nearly four years after commencing his mission to preach in *broken* English, or Anglo-Kusaien. He endeavored to teach the English in school, but he finally abandoned the experiment, and fell back upon the vernacular of the natives. He found it to be exceedingly difficult to communicate religious truths in this mixture of Kusaien, English, Spanish, Hawaiian and other languages. This same difficulty, we apprehend, would be still more manifest if the scheme should be generally undertaken of substituting the English language for Hawaiian, Tahitian or Samoan. We know that there are some innovators, who are very sanguine upon the point, that you can substitute English for Hawaiian, in all of our schools.

We do not believe it practicable even now, and much less when the missionaries first commenced their labors upon the Sandwich Islands. To substitute our language for another, among a rude and uncivilized people, is no easy undertaking. It would approach an impossibility to do it suddenly, or during a single generation. We are not aware as the history of the world presents any such example. There are parts of France, where we are informed that the old Celtic is spoken even now, while Gaelic is one of the written and spoken languages of the British Islands.

The difficulty attending the substitution of a foreign language for the vernacular of a people, is admirably illustrated in the attempt of William the Conqueror and his successors, to supplant the good old Anglo-Saxon by the French. The Norman conquest of England was accomplished in the eleventh century. William the Conqueror landed in England, A. D. 1066. During the three following centuries, no efforts were spared to banish the vernacular of the conquered people, but without success. The French, it is true, became the Court language, but the farmers, mechanics and common people, retained their mother-tongue. A similar result, we are confident, will attend a similar effort upon any of the islands of Polynesia. The French, at Tahiti, may teach a few of the islanders to speak à la Française, and some few of the better educated Hawaiians may learn to speak English, but the majority, we are confident, will always speak "their own tongue, wherein they were born." We would not assert that an Hawaiian cannot acquire a correct knowledge of the English language, for there are many who have surmounted every obstacle, and can now correctly speak and write the English language. There are but few if any English and American residents upon the islands, who can speak and write the English language with greater accuracy than his Majesty, Kamehameha IV.

While at Strong's Island, we were surprised in mingling among the natives to find so many of them who were able to speak in the *jargon* which has been thus introduced. Their ability to pronounce some of the difficult sounds of the English language was very remarkable. We tested their ability by requesting a native who had never left the island, to pronounce such words as Mississippi, Missouri, Shalmanezer and several other words in which sibilants abound. He could do it, with the utmost ease. We found the Caroline Islanders much more readily acquiring a knowledge of the English language, than the inhabitants of the Hawaiian Islands, who find it exceedingly difficult for their organs of speech to enunciate any words abounding with *hissing* sounds.

Mr. Snow is preparing a Grammar of the Kusaien language, which he finds to possess many peculiarities, which will be interesting to philologists. It is evidently a dialect of the same language as spoken by the Caroline Islanders generally, but totally unlike the language of Polynesians. It is a language abounding with words signifying deferential respect, for those in authority, especially for chiefs. "Your Honor," "Your Excellency," "My Lord," &c., &c., interlard the ordinary conversational intercourse of life. An Hidalgo from Old Spain, would probably find the Kusaiens fully equal to the genuine Castilians in the punctilios of conversation.

It was amusing, and rather suggestive, to witness a people living in filth and nakedness, debased to the very lowest degree in the social scale, still maintaining a species of refined intercourse, and delicate respect for one another. When they speak it is in a quiet undertone, very far removed from a rude, boisterous and hilarious turn of mind. They are seldom, if ever, known to engage in insolent and angry discussion. When one becomes angry with another, he does not vent his anger by outrageous language and violent blows, but quietly turns away, and refuses to speak with the offending party! A Kusaien can receive no greater insult than for a neighbor to refuse to speak to him! We asked Mr. Snow, how a Kusaien would exhibit his anger towards a person who had offended him? He replied, "by refusing to speak to him." If with us "silence gives consent," with the Kusaiens, "silence shows contempt."

XXXI.

KING GEORGE OF KUSAIE.

Long before the Missionaries landed upon Kusaie, or Strong's Island, through the reports of shipmasters and sailors, we had been made acquainted with King George. He was a very remarkable man, considering the circumstances of his birth and education. Capt. Jackson, of the whale ship *Inez*, makes the following remarks respecting King George: "The King is a man of good sense and sound judgment, possessing a large share of Indian cunning and craftiness; for instance, when I talked with him about their religion and smiled at some of their superstitious customs, he winked and said it was the fashion of Strong's Island, giving me to understand that he knew better." (See *Friend*, February, 1849.) This man often expressed a desire to have missionaries sent to Kusaie, and sincerely deplored the sad effects of the intercourse of his people with persons of abandoned character. Capt. Jackson's letter contains full particulars upon this subject.

On the arrival of the missionaries in 1852, King George received them with open arms. The Rev. Mr. Snow thus writes under date of Oct. 14, 1852: "Here I am on the much talked of island, and Mrs. Snow with myself and one of the Hawaiian families are to remain with the far-famed *King George*. In the early communications of the missionaries residing upon that island, there is very frequent and full mention of this King. He entered fully into the object of the mission and exerted his influence to promote its success. He caused a large church to be built and promoted the instruction of the young. As we have already stated, in Paper XXV, King George died in Sept. 9th, 1854, universally lamented by his people, and in the opinion of the missionary, a sincere believer in the gospel of our Lord and Saviour Jesus Christ.

In furnishing this brief notice of *King George* of Kusaie, we are reminded of another *King George*, even more remarkable, and worthy to be ranked among the most distinguished of all the Kings who have ever arisen and reigned in any of the islands of Polynesia. We refer to King George the present reigning King of Tonga, one of the Friendly Islands of the "South Seas," and local preacher in the Wesleyan Methodist Church. We are unable to state his age, but know that he has been King of that island over twenty years. He is known among all the South Sea Islands as a remarkable man, and wise ruler, while his fame has extended abroad to other parts of the world. Sir E. Home, commanding the British man-of-war, *Calliope*, thus refers to him in 1852: "I saw the noble and christian conduct of King George. He can only be compared to Alfred the Great, of blessed memory. He is worthy of being called a King. He is the greatest man in these seas."

"In November, Sir E. Home returned in the *Calliope* to the Friendly Isles, that he might learn the result of the visit of the French ship of war. He seemed very anxious that no harm should happen to the Friendly Islanders or the King. His visit was an occasion of much joy to all parties. However, the French ship had not arrived. But on the 12th of November, two days after Sir E. Home left Tonga, the *Moselle* made her appearance. Her commander, Captain Belland, was commissioned by the Popish governor of Tahiti to inquire into certain complaints lodged against King George by the captain of a French whaler, the *Gustave* of Havre-de-Grace, and also by the Romish priests residing in Tonga. The King obeyed the summons of the captain, and went on board the *Moselle*, taking witth him his state paper box, in which he had copies of all his correspondence, especially that with the Romish priests. The correspondence he laid before the captain, who viewed the King and his papers with astonishment. At the close of their long interview, which lasted five hours, and throughout which the King conducted himself with the greatest Christian propriety, the French captain expressed himself entirely satisfied, and stated to the King that "the French government, through him, acknowledged George as King of the Friendly Islands; and that the only condition he would impose was that, if any Frenchman chose to reside in his dominions, he should be protected, so long as he obeyed the laws; and that if any of the king's subjects chose to become Roman Catholics, they should be allowed to do so." To these conditions the King agreed, and the dreaded French war ship took her departure, the captain declaring that he "had seen and conversed with many chiefs in the South Seas, but that he had not seen one to be compared in knowledge and ability, in courage and dignity, to George, the King of the Friendly Islands."—(Cyclopedia of Missions.)

Our latest notice of King George is in the London *Watchman*, of August 1, 1861. Dr. Dobson, who had just returned from Australia, thus refers to King George; "And I have further to add, that King George, the Methodist Local Preacher of Tonga, asks counsel on the law of Divorce in his dominions." From this brief allusion, we learn that he is still alive and laboriously engaged in adjusting the civil and religious statutes of Tonga. When we know what Christianity has done for some of the chiefs and rulers of the Polynesian Islands, we cannot but express our regrets that the gospel should not have been made known among them until the 19th century.

XXXII.

A GLANCE AT THE CAROLINE ISLANDS.

Most of the islands or islets of this extensive range or Archipelago, are quite too small to find a place in any School Atlas, or even those maps which purport to embrace all the islands of the Pacific. The Caroline Archipelago is made up of no less than forty-eight small groups, and these groups contain nearly five hundred small islands. Of these five hundred islands, at most, there are but four or five high islands, hence this Archipelago contains nearly five hundred small coralline islets. The Russian navigator Lutke, makes the following significant remarks respecting these islands : " With the exception of the high Islands of Ualan, Ponapi, and Roug, if they were all collected together, and then placed above the spire of the fortress of Petropauloski, they would not hardly cover all St. Petersburgh and its suburbs. The length of all the islands joined together (I do not mean the reefs) would be 25 German miles ; the breadth of but very few of them exceeds 200 yards, and half of them are beneath this measurement."

It was our privilege to visit but two islands of this Archipelago, viz: Ualan, Kusaie, or Strong's Island, and Ascension, or Ponapi. Both of these are high islands. They are basaltic in their formation. From their productions, situation and good harbors, they have been much frequented by ships. They are the only islands upon which missionaries have become located. Missions were established upon both Ualan and Ponapi, in 1852, when the schooner *Caroline* made the first Missionary voyage to that portion of the Pacific.

Some of the Caroline Islands were discovered by the Spaniards in the 16th and 17th centuries. It is chiefly due to the Russian and French navigators, that we are indebted for surveys of these islands. Capt. Duperrey, in the French ship *La Coquelle*, in 1823, and Rear-Admiral Lutke, of the *La Seniavine*, thoroughly explored and surveyed some of these islands, including Ualan and Ponapi.

XXXIII.

ISLAND OF PONAPI, OR ASCENSION.

Two days after leaving Strong's Island, we caught a glimpse of Ponapi, but did not come to anchor until the next morning, June 23d. The *Morning Star* remained at anchor in the middle harbor, eleven days. During this period, it was our privilege to twice visit each of the Mission Stations at Kiti, (Rev. Mr. Sturges') and Shalong, (Rev. Mr. Roberts'.) By day and night, we cruised over the reefs, visited places of interest, and explored the far-famed ruins.

This island produces abundantly, yams, bread fruit, bananas, pine apples, squashes, sago, cocoanuts, arrow-root, sweet potatoes, and many other tropical productions. It is densely wooded and produces several varieties of excellent ship timber. We met at the island Capt. Newald of Boston, who was building a schooner of about 60 tons. He spoke of the ship-timber as of a most excellent quality. One species he called *Bermuda Cedar*, which is highly prized by the shipbuilders of England, and another species, much resembling the *Yatti* of Java, which is much prized in the East Indies. This island is well adapted to the cultivation of rice and sugar cane. It is the largest island of the Caroline Archipelago, being about fifty miles in circumference. It is surrounded by an extensive barrier reef, over which the surf breaks, three, six, eight and ten miles from the main land.

The forests abound with various tropical birds, including pigeons, parrots and a great variety of beautiful songsters. We have not heard such forest music for many years, as greeted our ears at the Rev. Mr. Sturges' Station. The sea abounds with a great variety of fish, and the reefs are peopled by an endless diversity of mollusks and shell fish. We do not believe any island of this vast ocean presents a more interesting field of exploration, for the botanist, conchologist, entomologist, or the adept in any department of the natural sciences.

XXXIV.
NIGHT OF TOIL AT PONAPI.

" *Twice* fifty months in slow succession fled,
By faithful hands the gospel lamp was fed :
Fervent in zeal, their labors knew no pause,
Yet still no wakening convert blessed the cause."

Elliot, the apostle to the Indians of New England, preached his first sermon among them in 1646, but gathered no church until 1660. Long was that night of toil and season of trial. The pioneer missionaries to the "South Seas," labored for nearly twenty years, before the light of morning broke upon their night of trial. At the end of sixteen years, a few converts were gathered, sufficient to occasion the remark, "In that one year they reaped the harvest of sixteen laborious seed-times, sixteen dreary and anxious winters, and sixteen unproductive summers." The first baptism, however, was not administered at Tahiti until 1819, twenty two years after the missionaries landed from the ship *Duff*. That was indeed a long night of toil, and long trial of the strength of the missionary's faith. The English Missionaries in New Zealand, under the patronage of the Church Missionary Society, labored and toiled for a period of nine years, before they were permitted to administer the rite of baptism to their first converts, and at the end of twenty years the missionries reported but eight baptized converts. During subsequent years the spread of Christianity was exceedingly rapid, for from 1839 to 1849, in one district, the number of baptisms reached 2,893.

The American missionaries on the island of Ponapi or Ascension, have been called to pass through a similar night of toil, and season of trial, although not so long. Messrs. Sturges and Gulick landed there in 1852, but it was not until within the past year that a church has been organized:

" Twice fifty months, in slow succesion fled,
By faithful hands the gospel lamp was fed,"

before they were permitted to welcome converts from among the Ponapians, around the sacramental table, and administer the rite of baptism.
That privilege was granted the Rev. Mr. Sturges, last autumn, when
he organized a church at Ronokiti, and another at Shalong. The former now numbers twelve members, (as many as our Saviour gathered
around him, at the end of his eventful life,) and the latter numbers six
members, all of whom are now walking circumspectly, while a few others are affording the gratifying evidences that their hearts have been
savingly wrought upon, by the influence of the Holy Spirit. A spiritual work has unquestionably been commenced among the Ponapians.
The missionary's heart has been made glad, and doubtless angels have
rejoiced over the conversion of more than one sinner among that dark
hearted and superstitious race. It remains to be seen, whether the good
work shall progress. It will not surprise us to learn that this work is
opposed by the chiefs and many of the people. Symptoms of opposition and annoyance have already been manifested. Some of these occurred about the time of our visit. There was a state of things among
the Ponapians, strikingly illustrative of the following philosophic remark of one of the English missionaries laboring in the "South Seas."
"It is found in the history of missions, that the most severe trials do
not generally occur till the gospel begins to take effect. So long as all
remains in the stillness of spiritual death, the missionary is generally
permitted to carry on his work with comparatively little molestation;
but when the power of divine truth begins to be felt on the heart, and
decided symptoms of spiritual life show themselves, then it is found
that the Lord of missions did not say in vain, 'Suppose ye that I am
come to give peace on earth: I tell you nay, but rather division.' "
These remarks were originally written with reference to the progress of
the missionary work on Aneiteum, one of the New Hebrides, but they
may yet apply with force to the work of missions in the North Pacific.
The friends of missions must not be surprised if such is the fact. (See
Cyclopedia of Missions, page 712.)

It may not be uninteresting to review the progress of the mission
upon Ponapi, or Ascension, and see if causes have not been operating
to produce a state of things indicated in the foregoing paragraphs.

Spanish navigators may have touched at Ponapi, as early as the
close of the 16th century, but the island could not have been said to be
discovered and explored until 1828, when visited by Lutke, of the
Russian Corvette, *La Seniavine*. (See Dr. Gulick's third Lecture.) From
that time to the present, the island has been repeatedly visited, and become the resort of whaleships. The inhabitants of Ponapi, from reading and observation, we should infer were of the Chinese and Malay
races intermingled, having scarcely any physiological or mental char-
acteristics in common with the Polynesian races. Intellectually we believe them to have been decidedly superior to Hawaiians or any Polynesian race which we have seen. Dr. Gulick remarks, in regard to them,
that "their minds are extremely inclined to suspiciousness and dis-
pleasure, but there seems to be no basis for the darker shades of sullen
moroseness. * * The Malayan trait of deception is carried on as far
as their loose characters permit."

They are divided into five tribes, the metes and bounds of which, are distinctly defined. Each tribe has its King and Chiefs, high and low. Among these tribes there is a deep rooted jealousy. Although the census of the island would now now number over five or six thousand, still the tribal laws are perpetuated, and so far as intercourse is maintained among the chiefs, much stately formality is observed, as appears in their feasts. There is no metropolitan or central government,—no London, or Paris, or Washington. From all we could learn, there is no tendency to union, but each tribe, and the rulers of each tribe choose to remain separate and distinct. We are not sure but the lines of the English poet will be found true when applied to Ponapians :

> —— "Mountains interposed,
> Make enemies of nations, who had else,
> Like kindred drops, been mingled into one."

The Ponapians do not even congregate in villages, but their houses are scattered, here and there, along the shores or through the forests, and around the bays. There existing several good harbors upon the island, ships have resorted thither for trading and obtaining supplies. From 1828 to 1852, vicious indulgences and immoral practices were carried on between the natives and low foreigners, with no one to utter a rebuke or interpose a remonstrance. Ascension became emphatically the "Paradise of beach-combers, alias *escapes* from Sydney, and runaway sailors." The influence of this class of persons among the people, was evil and only evil, and that continually. While visiting the Ronokiti Station, we called upon an old man, who had lived upon the island since 1832, or nearly thirty years. He was sick and approaching the end of life. We visited the poor old man three times, and conversed with him freely about the past. When asked, "What could have led you to settle among this people and live so long here?" his reply was, "to lead a life of laziness, drunkenness, debauchery and licentiousness." This answer told the whole story, and revealed the character of scores who have found a home upon Ascension. All the vices of civilization were rife there, so far as foreigners could introduce them among a degraded and heathen people. It was considered dangerous for ships to touch at some of the harbors.

Among such a people, and living under such influences, the American Mission was established in 1852. Hardly had the work been commenced, when, in 1854, the small pox appeared and not merely decimated the inhabitants as at the Sandwich Islands, but actually took every other man, woman and child, reducing the population more than one-half. It will readily be seen that the two missionaries, Messrs. Sturges and Gulick, commenced their work under circumstances as unpropitious and unfavorable as it is possible to conceive. The nation was reduced to its lowest state. This generation had inherited the terrible legacy of by-gone generations of superstition, vice and crime, to which was superadded a vast influx of foreign immoralities and vices, upheld and practiced by men devoid of shame, and impelled forward by the spirit of evil. If Christianity triumphs over so many counter influences, it must be the work of time, and the youthful soldiers of the

8

cross, need not be surprised if they are called upon to pray, watch and labor, through a long "night of toil." Blessed be God, there are indications, that that "night of toil is drawing to a close." There are indications of a dawning light. The *Morning Star*, has appeared, and it is to be hoped the Sun of righteousness will ere long make his appearance. It has been our privilege to visit that spot, where the elements of light and darkness are now struggling for the mastery. Our inquiry was,

> " Watchman ! tell us of the night,
> What its signs of promise are ?"

We heard the reply,

> "Traveler ! o'er you mountain's height,
> See that glory-beaming Star."

We asked again,

> " Watchman ! does its beauteous ray
> Aught of hope or joy fortell ?"

The cheering answer came,

> " Traveler, yes :—it brings the day,—
> Promised day to Israel."

XXXV.

HEATHEN DEGRADATION INDICATED BY THEIR LANGUAGE.

It is the remark of an eminent English writer, " To study a people's language will be to study *them*, and to study *them* at best advantage, when they present themselves to us under fewest disguises, most nearly as they are." The truth of this remark is as applicable to the study of the inhabitants of Polynesia as to the polished nations of Europe. In our efforts to arrive at a tolerably correct view of Micronesians, we found no better method, than to sit down with the missionaries, and question them upon their success in communicating with their people upon religious subjects. It is a comparatively easy matter to pick up a few words and phrases, sufficient to barter in knives, fish hooks, and cloth. The trader may do this, in a few hours, but it is a very different affair to take up a grammatical and accurate study of their languages, so that the missionary may be able to translate the Bible, compile school books, and compose hymns. This however is the missionary's principal work, but it is a work which yields a large reward. It introduces him to the very heart of the people. He sees their naked bodies with his eyes, but the study of their languages enables him to see their moral and spiritual nakedness and deformity. Their departure from God may be estimated by their language, agreeable to the words of our Saviour: " But those things which proceed out of the mouth come forth from the heart ; and these defile the man." Math. 15:18. " How can ye, being evil, speak good things, for out of the abundance of the heart the mouth speaketh." Matt. 12:34. A people's language must indicate their moral character. The missionary becoming intimately acquainted with the language of the heathen, is able to judge, as no other person can, not acquainted with their language, respecting the moral degradation of the heathen. While the languages of Micronesia and other heathen nations or tribes are destitute of words and phrases to convey correct ideas of God and moral subjects generally, yet those same languages abound with words and terms respecting disgusting subjects and forbidden thoughts. Their vocabularies are wonderfully prolific in unchaste and impure words and terms. How painfully the mind of the missionary is tried, when he would translate the Bible into the language of the heathen. He finds that their languages are wanting in the words and terms required for translation. These languages may once have possessed those necessary sounds and terms, but alas, so far have the heathen wandered from the right way, and so grievously have they departed from God, that they have lost correct ideas of the Divine Being and his worship. Hence, the missionary must spend toilsome days and sleepless nights, in his search after the proper terms, words and phrases to express religious truths. We found every missionary in Micronesia, eager in the study of the language of those islanders, where they are located, because there are now four American Missionaries in Micronesia, and each one is endeavoring to acquire the knowledge of what may be classified as a new language, for the inhabitants of Apaiang, Ebon, Kusaie, and Ponapi, speak really different languages, rather than different dialects of the same language.

The difficulty attending these labors of the missionary, is often very great. He will spend months and even years before he is able to fix upon some word that will correspond to the Bible idea which he wishes to convey. The Rev. Mr. Sturges, although nine years among the Ponapians, has not yet settled upon the proper and satisfactory word for *conscience*, in the Ponapian language. The Rev. Mr. Doane, although speaking the language of the Marshall Islanders with fluency, after a residence of four years upon Ebon, has not yet been able to ascertain if there is any word in that language which correctly conveys the idea of *regeneration or the new birth*. Mr. Sturges has been equally perplexed respecting the same word, but more recently, he hopes, that he has met with a term that conveys the idea, viz : *wilikap ata*. Wili signifiying *exchange*, Kap *new*, and *Ata* the directive. We asked him to inform us what a Ponapian understood by this term "Wilikap ata." He replied, that a native once illustrated the term thus,—" A person born anew or again, is the same as if a shriveled and decrepit old woman should suddenly become young again."

Thus the missionaries in Micronesia, are laboring in the same manner as the apostles did, respecting whom an English divine has remarked, that they " fetched from the dregs of paganism, words which the Holy Spirit has not refused to employ for the setting forth of the great truths of our redemption." The Greek word translated " regeneration," is a good illustration of this remark. This word, it was necessary, however, to convert from paganism to christianity—to *evangelize* it, if the term may be allowed! Long has **Mr.** Doane been laboring to fix upon some word to signify *repentance ;* but we need not produce other instances, for they have been continually occurring in the studies of every missionary not only in Micronesia and Hawaii, but every part of the heathen world where missionaries have gone. How little the unreflecting visitor can sympathize with the missionary in his labors and toils or *pilikias*, to employ a term of Hawaiian derivation rapidly gaining currency among foreigners in the Pacific, and which ere long may take its position beside *Tabu*, in Webster and Worcester. Viewing the labors of the missionary from this point of observation, he takes a position among the scholars and linguists of the world. Enter his sanctum, and you see spread out upon his table, lexicons, dictionaries, books of exegesis, manuscripts. Greek Testament, and by his side sits a native, who is continually plied with questions respecting the meaning of words and sounds of letters, and it would not be strange if the missionary's wife was called from her domestic duties in the nursery or kitchen to give her opinion upon the meaning of some word or phrase! Thus the missionary is employed in digging up *Greek roots,* examining *Hebrew points,* comparing *English and German dictionaries,* looking into *numerous commentaries,* and gathering information from every imaginable source, in order to translate the "Glorious gospel of the blessed God" into the language of the heathen to whom he has been sent. The eminent Dr. Judson, often lamented his want of books, dictionaries and other aids, in the work of translation. On one occasion, in writing to the Secretary of the Baptist Missionary Society in Boston, he thus remarks: "I frequently see a sterling work on the cover of the Herald or Magazine, and am ready to *scream* with variations, ' The Book, the Book, my kingdom for a Book!' Yes, a kingdom, if the same ship which brought the notice had brought the book too; whereas I have to wait for letters to cross the ocean twice or three times at least, and thus two or three years' use of the book is lost, during which time I am, perhaps, working upon that very portion of scripture which that book is intended to illustrate."

Who will not say that the missionary's life is a noble one, when thus employed? He is following in the foot-steps of Wickliffe, Tyndale and that glorious company of biblical scholars of the 17th century, who furnished our incomparable English version of the Bible. Thus Elliot toiled, and his translation of the Bible into the language of the Indians of Massachusetts, is a noble monument to his memory. Thus Judson toiled, and after forty years, gave the Bible in the vernacular to the Burmese. Thus we found the missionaries in Micronesia at their work. Toil on, Brethren! Our visit may not have benefited you, but it did us good. You are doing a good and noble work. If language is "the amber in which a thousand precious and subtle thoughts have been embedded and preserved," you are embedding heavenly and divine truths in the languages of Micronesia, which will be preserved long after your labors have ceased, and continue to guide immortal souls in the pathway toward heaven!

The following paragraph from a lecture of Prof. Trench, King's College, London, will show that Catholic Missionaries, in South America, meet with the same leading facts among the heathen, that we have referred to in the labors of Protestants.

" Dobrizhoffer, the Jesuit Missionary, in his curious History of the Abipones, tells us that neither they nor the Guarinnies, two of the principal native tribes of Brazil, with whose language he was intimately acquainted, possessed any word which in the least corresponded to our 'Thanks.' But what wonder if the feeling of gratitude was entirely absent from their hearts, that they should not have possessed the corresponding word in their vocabularies? Nay, how should they have had it there? And that this is the true explanation, is plain from a fact which the same writer records, that although inveterate askers, they never showed the slightest sense of obligation, or of gratitude, when they obtained what they sought; never, saying more than, 'This will be useful to me,' or 'This is what I wanted.'" We would merely add, that similar remarks have we heard again and again from Protestant Missionaries in the Sandwich Islands and Micronesia.

XXXVI.

HONESTY IS THE BEST POLICY; OR DISHONESTY THE WORST POLICY.

This oft-quoted old English proverb, finds facts in abundance to corroborate its truth. It is not only true when applied to the dealings of men in civilized and christian lands, but to the dealings of those from civilized and christian lands who go among savages for the purposes of barter and trade. In our intercourse among the inhabitants of Micronesia, this fact was painfully impressed upon us, by too many sad examples of injustice and dishonesty, that honesty and fair dealing has not been the rule which has guided the civilized man in his traffic and dealings with the savage. Instances of well attested fraud and meanness, are commonly reported in those regions, which if brought before a jury of twelve honest men, would send the perpetrators to the State prison, or transport them to the penal colonies of Australia. Take the following as an example: a certain shipmaster in his dealings with the natives of the Marshall Islands, agreed to pay a certain amount of tobacco, but what does he give in its place?—*pieces of old tarred rope, cut up to correspond to the length of plugs of tobacco!* That man may have thought he had done a smart thing, and drove a profitable trade, but only think of the meanness and guilt of the infamous transaction. Hanging with a piece of tarred rope, would be too lenient a punishment for such guilty meanness. Think of the enmity which one such act would excite and keep alive among those savages! No wonder their policy has been one of blood and murder towards the white man. Take another example. The inhabitants of Ebon, one of the Marshall Islands cut off a California schooner in 1852. Among the spoils, they found gold. It can be proved that it was not the chiefs, but some of the common people, who committed this act of piracy. The chiefs however took the money. A certain ship master touches at Ebon, and finds this gold among the people. He obtains several hundred dollars in gold, and promises to pay in tobacco, but getting the gold into his possession, makes sail and leaves the island. He doubtless reasons, those islanders are pirates and robbers; they have no right to this money! But what right had that shipmaster? Had he any better claim than that of a robber and a pirate? If that shipmaster was an Englishman or American, we ask him to ponder this proverb, " *The receiver is as bad as the thief.*" If he was a Frenchman, let him ponder a proverb to be found in his language, which translated into English, reads thus : " *He sins as much who holds a sack, as he who puts into it.*"

Respecting another shipmaster, who formerly cruised in that region and took away from Ebon some of the gold referred to, we would remark that he came to a most untimely fate. A correspondent of the *Friend* thus wrote from Ascension, Feb. 19, 1853: "Captain ——, of the *William Penn* received, it is said, over a thousand dollars. It was for this money one of his crew, an Oahu native killed him. That native has since been killed on Simpson's Island, by one, it is said, whom he himself was about to shoot. Thus do the dead bury their dead, and murderers execute murderers." (See *Friend* for July, 1853.)

We might multiply examples, almost without end, of the base tricks and little meannesses, dishonest bargains and dishonorable dealings of the white man with the savage or the inhabitants of Micronesia. Perhaps no islanders have ever fared worse, at the hands of the white man, than the New Zealanders, at the hands of Sydney traders and whalers. We quote the following from an English book, entitled "The Southern Cross and Southern Crown, or the Gospel in New Zealand :"

"A little incident occurred one day when dining with a large party at Government House, [Sydney in 1806,] showing Tippahee's shrewdness of observation, and courage in expressing his opinion. [Tippahee was a New Zealand chief, who was visiting Port Jackson, Sydney.] A discussion arose as to our penal code: he could not reconcile our punishment of theft, with his own sense of justice, maintaining that stealing food when perhaps the chief was hungry, ought not to be severely punished. He was told in reply, that according to English law every man who took the property of another was liable to be put to death. 'Then,' exclaimed he, with animation, addressing the Governor, 'why do you not hang Captain ——, [pointing to a gentleman then at the table.] Captain, he came to New Zealand, he come ashore and tiki (steal) my potatoes ; you hang Captain ——.' The captain was covered with confusion, for the charge was true ; he had, when off the coast and in want of potatoes, sent a boat's crew on shore, dug up Tippahee's plantation and carried off the the produce without offering him the slightest remuneration." Would that this was the only similar instance which might be quoted. How many such instances have tended to rouse the enmity of New Zealanders, and it may be true, that could the full history of the intercourse of Englishmen with the New Zealanders, be written out, it would be found that instances of wrong and injustice occurring a half century ago, were so *burnt into* the souls of the New Zealanders, that they are remotely the cause of that relentless war now raging between New Zealanders and

English soldiers. We now recall to mind the story of an Englishman, from New Zealand, related in our hearing some years ago. In a former war, the seat of which was the Bay of Islands, the natives were off their guard and unprepared for an attack, because it was the Christian Sabbath! They were told that *Christian soldiers* would not make an attack upon that day! Alas, that was the day when they rushed in and butchered the unsuspecting savages!—(See Southern Cross, &c., page 226.)

While referring to "the tricks of traders," we recall to mind the instance of a certain shipmaster, (and we could give name of ship and master,) who purchased furs of an Indian in Plover Bay, Arctic Ocean, and agreed to pay *in rum*, but so adroitly was the Indian deceived, that he took ashore a *keg of salt water!* As if dealing in rum was not sufficiently bad, but the mean souled man must put salt water into the keg, in place of the rum!! What would not such a man do for money! We frequently met that man in the streets of Honolulu. He acknowledged the deed, but tried to apologize for its baseness. We asked him, could you blame those Indians, if they cut off the next ship which entered their Bay for trade or supplies? He replied not a word, and we parted. When we reflect upon such instances of guilty meanness and dishonorable baseness, we are inclined to ask, when hearing of ships cut off in Micronesia and elsewhere, "have not the guilty perpetrators cause for resentment?"

If shipmasters and traders, going among savages, are not influenced by the precept of our Saviour, "Do unto others, as ye would they should do unto you," it is strange that they cannot be induced to act from the principle of self-preservation. If they are not, very soon some of their seafaring companions may be cast ashore wrecked among those savages. If they are, what *but death* can they expect will be their fate?

There is current among the free blacks of Hayti, a proverb, which we would commend to the consideration of those who are inclined to deal dishonestly with savages—"*Before crossing the river, do not curse the crocodile's mother,*" meaning, provoke not wantonly those into whose power you presently may be cast.

While alluding to these instances of dishonorable conduct, on the part of the white man, with his savage brother of a darker skin, it affords us pleasure to record the fact, that many have pursued an opposite course. The savage appreciates honesty and fair dealing. When traders and shipmasters pursue an honorable and upright course, they are remembered and their second visit will be hailed with joy, but if a trader of the opposite character ever returns, let him beware of the consequences. The trouble is, the innocent are made to suffer for the guilty, as at the Marshall Islands and other localities.

A most remarkable illustration of the remark that "the innocent are made to suffer for the guilty," we have in the murder of the Rev. John Williams, the Apostle of Polynesia and Martyr of Erumanga. We copy the following from the Samoan *Reporter* for March, 1860. The Rev. George Turner, in reporting the 14th voyage of the Missionary bark *John Williams*, makes the following statements respecting his visit to Erumanga, on Saturday, 15th of October, 1859:

" Anchored in Dillion's Bay on the following morning, viz., Saturday, Oct. 15th. Mr. Gordon was soon on board, and accompanied by him some of us went ashore, and up the hill to his residence, about 1,000 feet above the level of the sea, and there we found Mrs. Gordon well. Owing to the unhealthy swamps on the low grounds, Mr. G. has built his cottage on the high land. Close by the house, he has erected a small chapel, and has a fine bell at the one end, which echoes from hill, to hill, and calls the tribes to their little Zion.

" Every spot was associated with the tragic scenes of November, 1839. At the foot of the hill on which the chapel stands is the stream in which Mr. Harris fell, and the beach where Mr. Williams ran into the sea. Down the hill, below Mr. Gordon's study window, is the spot where the oven was made in which Mr. Williams' body was cooked. Over in another direction is the place where the body of Mr. Harris was taken. Inland is a grove of cocoanuts, underneath one of which the skull of Mr. Williams was buried. The bones taken to Samoa by Capt. Croker, in H. M. S. *Favourite* in 1840, were *not* the remains of Williams and Harris. He had no proper interpreter. The natives thought he wanted to *buy human bones*, and took off for sale whatever were handy from one of the adjacent caves, where they deposit their dead. One of the skulls was that of the father of a lad we had for some time with us in our Institution in Samoa. It is difficult at present, owing to hostility among the tribes, to get at the precise tree under which the skull of Mr. Williams was buried; but there let the remains of the martyr rest, and form part and parcel of the root of that palm which waves its foliage in every breeze, emblematic of the Christian hero's triumph! A piece of red sealing-wax found in Mr. W.'s pocket was supposed by the natives to be some portable god, and was carefully buried near where the skull was laid. · Mr. Gordon lately recovered this, and handed it to me, to convey to Mr. W.'s children, as the only relic which he has been able to obtain of their lamented father. At first he thought, from the description of the native, that this ' god' would turn out to be Mr. W.'s *watch*; but when found, it was only red sealing-wax. The clothes and other things found on the body after the massacre, were all distributed about, with the exception of this bit of sealing-wax, an inch and a half-long.

"We had the pleasure of spending a Sabbath at Erumanga, and met with about 150 of the people in their little chapel. All were quiet and orderly. It thrilled our inmost soul to hear them, as led by Mr. Gordon, strike up the tune of New Lydia, and also the translation and tune of ' There is a happy land.' Mr. Macfarlane and I addressed them through Mr. Gordon. They were startled and deeply interested as I told them of former times, when we tried so hard to get intercourse with them, and to show them that we were different from other white men who had visited their shores. When I read out the names of seven who swam off to us in 1845, and to whom we shewed kindness, and took on shore in the boat, it appeared, from the sensation created, that one of them was present. He came, after the service, shook hands, said some two or three more of them were alive, that our visit that day greatly surprised them, and that they marked our vessel as the one which shewed them kindness, and did not take sandal-wood. They thought us quite different from all the white men with whom they had previously came in contact.

"On the Saturday, I saw and shook hands with the chief Kauiau. who killed Mr. Williams, and on Monday met with him again. I also saw one of his men, called Oviallo, who killed Mr. Harris.— These two men feel ashamed and shy when the *John Williams* comes. Neither of them was at the service on Sabbath. Probably they have had a fear also which they found it difficult to shake off. I hope, however, that Kauiau has *now* perfect confidence in our friendly intentions. On the Monday, he and Oviallo walked about with us, shewed us the place where Mr. Harris was first struck, the place in the stream a few yards from it where he fell, and the course along the road, and down to the beach where Mr. Williams ran right into the sea. Here, too, Oviallo helped us to pick up some stones to take with us as mementoes to surviving friends of the sad event. Mr. Gordon has erected a little printing-office and teacher's residence close to the spot where the first blow was struck at Mr. Harris. I have planted a date palm seed there, in a line towards the stream with the spot where Mr. Williams fell.

" But the most striking and permanent memento of that sad day is a great flat block of coral on the road up the hill, about a gunshot from the place where Mr. Williams fell. There the natives took the body, laid it down, and cut three marks in the stone, to preserve the remembrance of its size. The one mark indicates the length of the head and trunk, and the other the lower extremities, thus :

| Head and trunk, | Extremities, |
| 37 inches. | 25 inches. |

A native lay down on the spot, and, lying on his right side, with his knees somewhat bent, said, that was how it was measured.

" When the *Camden* hove in sight, on that morning of the 20th of November, '39, the Erumangas thought it was a sandal-wooding party returned, who *had but recently killed a number of their people, and plundered their plantations.* They were the more confirmed in this impression from the fact that the boat pulled in to the very place where that party had landed before, and erected some huts. That morning, they had all ready prepared heaps of yams and taro for a feast which was to take place close by up the river; *they felt galled at the thought of their being stolen by the white men,* and determined to try and prevent their landing; or, if they did land, to attack them if they attempted to go up the river to the place where the yams and taro were. They sent the women and children out of the way, and hid themselves in the bush, but especially off the road leading up along the western bank of the stream. When Mr. Harris made to go up there, and had reached the spot where I have planted the palm tree, the shell blew, Kauiau rushed out with his party, and commenced the attack. Five out of seven who were foremost in the massacre are dead. The people were not united in the affair; some were for it, and some were against it; hence the remark of Capt. Morgan: 'They made signs for us to go away.' But the principal thing in that sad day which melted their hearts with pity

9

was, they say, 'the man in the boat who stood and wrang his hands and wept;' and that, I suppose, was good Capt. Morgan.

"After surveying these scenes, so full of affecting recollections, we went off to the vessel, and took Kauiau with us. We got him down into the cabin, and, as this is the first time he has ventured to go below, it proves that he has *now* entire confidence in us. We exchanged presents also. We gave him a trifle, and he and the people brought off to the ship forty yams, twenty heads of taro, and three bunches of bananas—the first present which the missionary vessel has ever had from Erumanga, and the murderer of John Williams. On showing Kauiau all over the ship, we stood before Mr. Williams' portrait in the saloon, and told him *that* was the missionary he killed. He gazed with intense interest, said he thought he could recognize the full face, and the stout body, and was earnest in leading up to it some others who were with him, and in explaining what it meant. Kauiau is still a heathen comparatively. Let us hope that he may soon take a stand on the side of Christ. Mr. Gordon says, that Oviallo is a more hopeful character, and seems to be deeply grieved as he thinks of his having had a hand in killing 'a man of God.' "

Thus it appears that the apostle to *Polynesia*, was murdered on account of the iniquitous and wicked conduct of sandal · wood traders. " If honesty is the best policy," so " dishonesty is the worst policy."

XXXVII.

EVERY MISSIONARY TO THE HEATHEN SHOULD BE A PHYSICIAN.

This should be the standing rule, and the only exception allowed should be in those instances when the missionary goes to parts of the world where there are educated physicians. We have not formed this opinion hastily. Some four years ago, at our suggestion, it was discussed at length in the meetings of the Hawaiian Evangelical Association, and the subject was deemed of sufficient importance to be noticed in the annual " general letter " to the Prudential Committee of the American Board in Boston.

We have seen the importance of medical knowledge and information among the missionaries upon these islands, but during our late cruise through Micronesia, the subject has been impressed by a wider range of observation. While at Apaiang, we witnessed the praiseworthy effort of the Rev. Mr. Bingham, to introduce vaccination. Eight days before our arrival he had visited the whale ship *Belle*, Capt. Brown, and obtained some excellent vaccine matter from the arm of Capt. B's infant child. The evening before our departure from Apaiang, Mr. Bingham, Capt. Gelett, and another person present, undertook the work of vaccination. We hope our humble efforts may prove as successful as those of Dr. Jenner, who first discovered the wonderful antidote to the small-pox, but never did we feel so much the importance of medical knowledge. Mr. Bingham laments his deficiency in this respect. Medical knowledge would increase his influence and usefulness, we verily believe, at least twofold. The Hawaiian Missionaries on Tarawa, are not supposed to know much about curing bodily diseases, yet applications are made to them for medical advice!

At the Marshall Islands, this subject was forced upon our consideration by a most painful combination of facts. There was sickness in the missionary's family, but no physician was at hand. There was sickness among the people, but there was no physician who felt confidence in his ability and skill, yet Mr. Doane was continually *compelled* to administer medicines and prescribe remedies. Mr. Doane felt so strongly upon the subject, that even now, at the age of thirty-six or seven, he is contemplating a visit to the United States for the purpose of attending a course of Medical Lectures.

During our detention at Kusaie, or Strong's Island, the same subject came up for consideration. Mr. Snow has been obliged to administer medicines. He is living among a diseased people. With medical knowledge, he might not have been able to have saved a wasting race, but he might have enjoyed the satisfaction of having made an intelligent effort. He has done what he could, but often has been obliged to administer medicines, when medical knowledge might have led him to have acted differently. The natives will have medicines. They are believers in the art! King George's favorite son was dangerously sick a few years ago, and a whaler arrived in port. The king hurried for medicine. The shipmaster gave him a bottle of *something*, and the following morning, the young man was a corpse. The King was heard to remark, " Well, the Captain's intentions were good."

On our arrival at Ponapi, we very soon became acquainted with facts in abundance, to show the importance of medical knowledge among missionaries. What would not the Rev. Mr. Sturges have given for medical knowledge during the ravages of the small pox? The following is an extract from his journal, published in the *Missionary Herald* for May, 1855 :

" *July* 12, 1854. The Lord's hand is heavy upon us. Never did death work more fearfully, or with less opposition. The panic-struck natives fly to the mountains and to uninhabited islands; then they come back again, and seize some victim of the disease to carry to their homes, thus spreading the contagion to all parts, so that a spot cannot be found where it is not doing fearful execution. Never was desolation more complete.

" Nor is it a small ingredient in our bitter cup, that we can do no more to lessen the evil. Our destituton of vaccine matter, the power of the priests over a bigoted people, together with the stories of abandoned foreigners respecting our bringing the sickness here and our intention to kill all the natives, render our efforts to come into contact with their sufferings nearly fruitless. They often resort to the basest deceptions to keep us from the dwellings of the sick, that the additional curse of our presence may not fall upon them. Much has been said to them about inoculation ; but they do not understand its nature ; and as it would kill some, and serve to spread the contagion, it seems a matter of prudence not to press it.

" In these circumstances, with the dying groans of thousands in our ears, forced by heathen superstition and a heathenized civilization from sufferings which we would gladly mitigate, shut out from all connection with a Christian world, we love to think of the thousands who remember us at the throne of grace. It is sweet to go there often ourselves, and to those rich promises, 'They that sow in tears shall reap in joy;' 'Lo, I am with you always.'

"20. For weeks I have been mostly confined to our own district, going about but little, as our Nanakin keeps his people at their homes, allowing but little intercourse, wishing to keep the sickness at a distance. This is a large district, and nearly the only one where the small-pox has not made ravages.

"During this temporary seclusion, the Nanakin, with his train, has been quite attentive to his books, coming to my house every day for instruction. "Besides my ordinary teaching, I have tried to communicate some things respecting the treatment of the small-pox to the people through him; and I hope I have not utterly failed. He would, no doubt, request to be inoculated, were it not for the fears of others. We rejoice, and would have our friends rejoice with us, in a more unobstructed and friendly contact with this suffering, deluded people."

SUCCESSFUL INOCULATION.—As Mr. Sturges has not received a medical education, it will be seen in the following extract that he assumed a very grave responsibility. There are few men who would not shrink from such a measure.—(*E l. of Missionary Herald.*)

"*August* 5. I have this day inoculated our Nanakin. This is decidedly the greatest venture of my life. If he does well, all will be well; if he dies, we can hardly expect to escape savage violence. We try to work the Lord's will; and we know he always makes issues for the highest good.

"12. I have this day re-inoculated the Nanakin, and with him a favorite brother. This shows his determination, and his confidence in the missionary. Never did I feel more the need or help of special pleadings with the great Physician than now.

"25. These anxious weeks are over. The Nanakin is well, having had the sickness so lightly that it is hard to feel he has been sick. His brother also is doing well. To the Lord let all glory be given! I am now very busy inoculating. Every body, far and near, urges me to this. I have now, and shall have for weeks, more than I can do. Poor people! Some of them will die, probably many, and I must have the credit of killing them. I do sometimes tremble at my responsibilities; but I will never shrink, so long as I can feel that the hand of my Master is about me. The Nanakin accompanies me in my visits to distant parts of the tribe. This he does that I may not have to propel my own canoe, and to give more influence."

Another extract will indicate the hazard of medical practice among such a people. It will also illustrate the mastery which superstition has gained over them.—(*Ed. Missionary Herald.*)

"*September* 10. A high chief, a subject of inoculation, has just died. He was one of the worst men we had, occasioning nearly all the wars between the tribes, as also robberies, neighborhood quarrels, &c. He urged the killing of the missionary, awhile since, as the cause of the sickness. Failing in this he fled to a small island, where he remained for months, until the small-pox broke out on his premises on the main land, when he returned. Seeing me inoculate the Nanakin, he begged with tears that I would do the same thing for him. Through all his sickness he was anxious to see me, as he seemed to have the greatest dread of dying. He might have lived; but at the crisis of his disease, the spirits appeared, saying, 'Come away,' 'Come away.' On receiving this order, he was carried several miles, which was too much for his weak body. Such orders for a change of place are almost always given in the later stages of sickness, and doubtless cause many deaths. Many are unquestionably buried alive. There are frequent cases of persons rising from their grave-clothes. This fact suggested to them the return of the soul to the body, after a temporary absence. They hurry the corpse into the ground, to keep any stranger from looking upon it, as this would greatly offend the spirit. All the fears of the living seem to center in the agency of departed spirits. If one is sick, or meets with any calamiity ; if any noise is heard at night; if anything singular happens, it is the work of ghosts."

Such facts, as the foregoing, are sufficient to convince any candid mind that a missionary to Micronesia, should be a physician as well as clergyman. There are very many other missionary fields where the call is equally pressing for missionary physicians. We do think the Board of Missions in Boston, should insist that missionary candidates should have attended, at least, one course of Medical Lectures. We can anticipate some of the excuses or pleas which will be offered for neglecting the study of medicine by missionary candidates—viz:' want of time, pecuniary means, disinclination, &c. Then we reply, the Board should make the rule imperative and stringent. It would be a saving of money to the Board, in the end, if every missionary candidate was educated as a Physician from the funds of the Missionary Society.

An eminent Frenchman, gives the following as his definition of a physician : " An unfortunate gentleman who is expected every day to perform a miracle, namely, to reconcile health with intemperance."

But the missionary, without medical knowledge, is still more unfortunate, for he is expected to arrive at the same result, but must go at his work blindly!

The following extract from the "Cyclopedia of Missions," presents our *beau ideal* of the method of carrying on the work of missions among a heathen people:

" *Arcot.*—This city is seventy miles from Madras, on the road to Bangalore, and is the centre of a very populous and destitute district. At this place Mr. M. Scudder commenced a mission in March, 1850. Having already become quite distinguished for his medical and surgical skill, his services were in immediate demand, from forty to fifty visiting him daily. His custom was to meet his patients in the morning, read and explain a passage of Scripture, and pray with them, after which he attended to their maladies. Through his medical labors he gained access to many Hindoo women, who could not have been reached in any other way. A regular dispensary was established, and Mrs. Scudder, who could speak Tamil, fluently visited it daily to converse with the patients."

Remarkable Ruins on the Island of Ascension, at the Metalanim Harbor, built entirely of Basaltic Prisms.

Surveyed by J. T. Gulick.

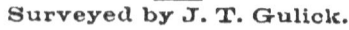

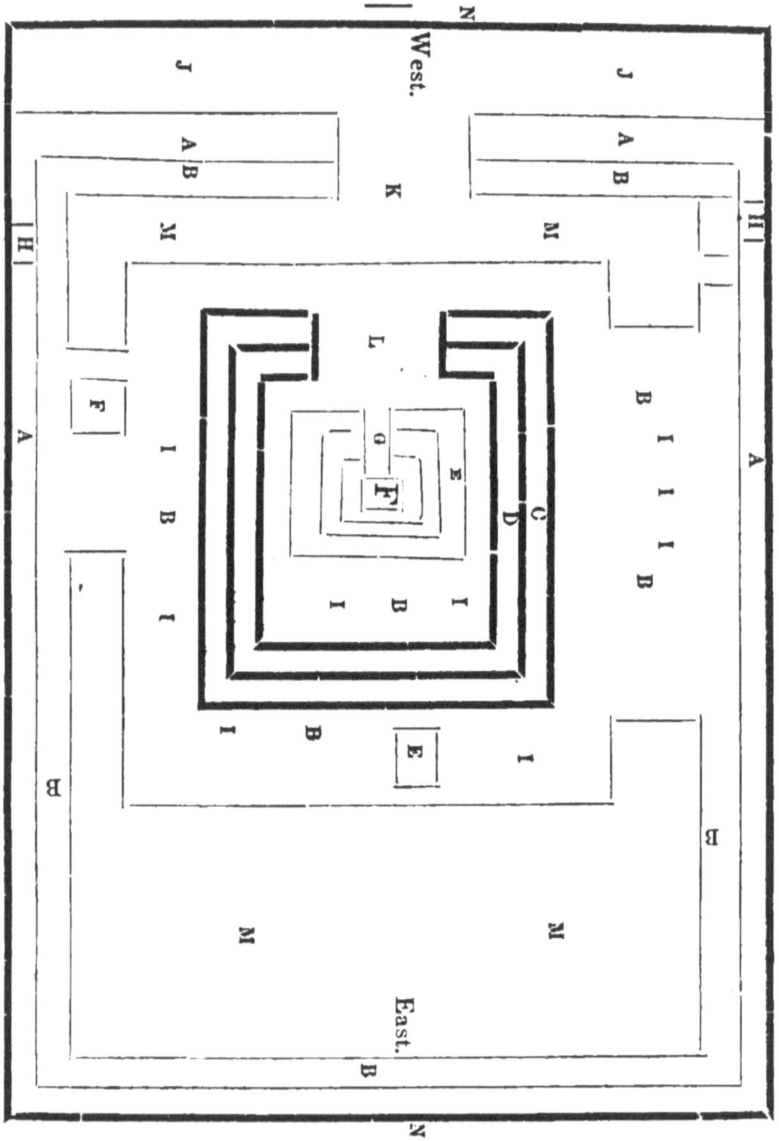

N

West.

East.

N

A The outer wall.
B The platform.
C The inner wall.
D The platform of the inner wall.
E Large steps to a platform over the centre vault.
F Vaults.

G Entrance into the centre vault; but now blocked up.
H Low passages through the walls.
I The position of several vaults, dimensions not known.
J The platform in front.

K The entrance through the outer wall.
L The entrance through the inner wall.
M The main platform, the same height as the platform in front.
N Water surrounding it.

XXXVIII.

RUINS ON PONAPI.

In former years we have published several articles upon the ruins on Ascension or Ponapi, as our readers may learn by referrng to the *Friend*, for December 17, 1852, and August 26th, 1857. Every person visiting the island, should not by any means leave without taking a look at these remarkable ruins. In extent and regularity, they far exceed those upon Kusaie. The ruins were first discovered by a sailor by the name of James F. O'Connell, who was wrecked in the English whale ship *John Bull* about the year 1827 or '28. This man resided several years upon the island, and subsequently escaped and finally found his way to Boston. There he found friends, who listened to the story of his adventures and published a volume, entitled, "*A Residence of eleven years in New Holland, and the Caroline Islands* ; being the Adventures of James F. O'Connell, edited from his verbal narrative; published by B. B. Mussey, Boston, 1836."

This volume contains much information respecting that island, and is deserving of perusal by any one who wishes to acquaint himself with the Caroline Islands. O'Connell was an Irishman by birth, and was naturally possessed of those mental traits which render the natives of the Emerald Isle, so celebrated. He must have possessed a remarkable memory, a quickness of perception and no ordinary powers of observation. While at Ascension, we met with an old resident, who remembered O'Connell, when he was a resident upon the island.

The foregoing sketch of the ruins, we republish from the *Friend* of December, 1852.

The Rev. E. W. Clark, who visited the ruins in 1852, thus describes his visit :

" They are situated upon low land extending out upon the flats which surround this island. We approached them from the inland side by crossing a creek or canal 20 or 30 feet wide, walled on both sides and nearly dry in low tide. This led us to the outer entrance of the ruins or fortifications, which was through a large open gateway. On Inspection, we found these ruins to consist of two quadrangular walls, one within the other. The length and breadth of the outer quadrangle, by a rough measurement, was 236 by 162 feet, and the wall from 6 to 10 feet thick, and in some places 25 feet high on the outside. This wall seemed entire in some places and in others broken and overgrown with vines and trees. Proceeding a few paces from the outer wall we came to the entrance of the inner enclosure facing the entrance to the outer. In front of the inner wall is a raised platform 10 or 12 feet wide. The inner wall was about 14 feet high, where it was not broken down, and 6 feet thick. The top rows of basaltic prisms of which this wall was built, projected over about two feet on the outside, apparently to prevent the walls being scaled from without. This inner enclosure was about 95 feet by 75 on the outside. In the center a little raised above the surrounding ground, was a large vault. The ancient entrance to it was thoroughly closed by basaltic prisms, but I entered through a crevice in the top. The vault I found to be about 15 feet by 10 inside, and 7 or

8 feet deep. The bottom was uneven, having been dug up apparently by former visitors in search of treasure or curiosities. The top of this vault was covered with immense basaltic columns extending the whole length and measuring 17 feet. On the top of the vault a large bread-fruit tree was growing, whose roots extended down through the vault to the ground below.

" There are several similar vaults in different parts of the ruins, mostly between the inner and outer walls. Human bones, I believe, have been found in some of them. Small pieces of ancient coin, a silver crucifix and a pair of silver dividers, have been found ; also a small brass cannon far inland. These were probably left here by Spanish adventurers long before the island was known to the civilized world."

We are unable to add much that would be of interest respecting these ruins. Their origin, and the motive prompting their builders, are unknown to the present inhabitants. We have no idea they were built for warlike purposes, but rather for those of superstition, or as burial places. They were far more extensive than we anticipated. We would refer our readers to Dr. Gulick's admirable article in the *Friend* for August, 1857.

XXXIX.

APPEAL IN BEHALF OF THE MICRONESIAN MISSION.

On our return from Micronesia, we preached a sermon in the Bethel. Sabbath morning, August 16th, from which we make the following extracts :

Text—"And when they [Paul and Barnabas] were come [to Antioch] and had gathered the church together, they rehearsed all that God had done with them, and how he had opened the door of faith unto the Gentiles."—Acts. xiv : 27.

In referring to the state of heathenism in Micronesia, we improved the occasion to speak of *the blessings of a well ordered civil government, and of the Family Institution.* Illustrations of the opposite were cited from scenes witnessed during our cruise.

" If we contrast the condition of the inhabitants of the islands of Micronesia with the condition of those living in civilized and Christian communities, no well balanced mind would hesitate to decide in favor of the latter. I have already carried out the contrast in reference to civil government, and the marriage or family institution. I might also continue the contrast, with reference to schools of every grade from the infant school to the university ; I might refer to all those social, literary and religious privileges and blessings which are so highly prized by all intelligent, moral and religious people. In speaking of these blessings, I might ask which of them do the Micronesians enjoy ? The contents of a mail-bag, they have eaten for food ! Eat for food ! In their ignorance, degradation and destitution, they have no disposition to rise to a higher rank than their fathers, and their fathers lived and died more like the brutes that perish, than like rational, accountable and immortal beings. Shall the inhabitants of those islands have the gospel preached among them ? Shall those blessings which Christians and those living in Christian lands so highly prize, be offered to them, or shall they be left as they have hitherto been, to dwell in ignorance, vice, and degradation, and pass onward to the bar of God, where we and they must stand ? How shall we meet them, and be able to answer for it, that while the Bible was in our hands and the means were in our possession, we did not do all in our power to convey to them the inestimable blessing ?

" Having been permitted the privilege of making this cruise along the shores of heathendom, and cast an eye into its dark domain,—having been privileged to see with my own eyes, that, through the efforts of a few missionaries, God has most wonderfully and widely ' opened the door of faith unto the Gentiles,' I return to plead the cause of missions, and urge upon Christians of every name and denomination, their duty to cause the gospel of our Lord and Saviour Jesus Christ, to be preached without delay among the Micronesians, Polynesians and all unenlightened and unevangelical nations. My language shall be that of our Saviour, when he declared, ' Say not ye, There are yet four months, and then cometh the harvest ? behold I say unto you, Lift up your eyes and look on the fields : for they are white already to the harvest. And he that reapeth receiveth wages, and gathereth fruit unto life eternal, that both he that soweth and he that reapeth may rejoice together.'—John iv: 35:36.

"There are many considerations why every reasonable effort should now be made to cause the gospel to be immediately published among the dwellers upon the islands of Micronesia, and all those portions of Polynesia, which are as yet unevangelized. English Christians have vigorously prosecuted the work of evangelization among the islands of the South Seas—group after group has been won over to the dominion of the Prince of Peace. Tahitians, Samoans, Tongans, and Feegeeians have successively arrayed themselves under the gospel banner. The savage inhabitants of the Solomon Group, and New Guinea, remain however to test the faith, try the zeal and combat the ardor of British Missionaries. Marquesans, after having virtually driven from their shores British and American Christian missionaries, have finally been compelled to ground the weapons of their spiritual warfare, and lay down their arms at the feet of Hawaiian soldiers of the cross. The Hawaiian Islanders have long since concluded to range themselves on the side of Christian nations. The effort is now being made to push the conquests of the cross westward. As is well known, missionaries are now laboring upon Apaiang, Tarawa, Ebon, Kusaie and Ponapi. They have obtained not only a foot-hold, but already a harvest is being gathered. Four months do not remain, ere sheaves shall be gathered. The process of sowing and reaping is going forward together. The sower going forth scattering the gospel seed, is compelled to grasp the sickle and gather in the sheaves. The present seems emphatically to be the favored and critical moment for prosecuting the work of missions which has been so auspiciously commenced upon the Gilbert and the Marshall Islands. Hawaiian missionaries can there work to good advantage, and those now upon the ground are nobly co-operating with missionaries from America. The difficulty is, that the mission is feeble in numbers, but those few are accomplishing an Herculean work. They should be reinforced without delay. More American and Hawaiian missionaries are called for and an open door of usefulness invites them to enter the field. No youthful missionary preacher or school teacher could ask or desire a more promising or inviting field. I envy not the man, who can visit that portion of the heathen world, from which I have returned, and gaze upon the thronging groups of children and crowds of adults, and not say 'mine eye affecteth my heart.' As I visited those crowded villages, in company with the missionaries, and saw the work to be done and the encouragement to labor in that work, I could sympathize with those missionaries as they raised the Macedonian cry, 'Come over, and help us.' They need help and they should have it. I pledged them my word that I would return, and do all in my power to send that help, and support both those now upon the ground and as many more as can be sent thither. The Micronesian Mission, I know, is under the patronage of the American Board of Missions, but that organization desires the cordial co-operation of Christians and the friends of missions upon these islands. That society is desirous that Hawaiian Christians will send forth a goodly number of missionaries. Those Hawaiian Missionaries, now upon Apaiang, Tarawa, and Ebon, are laboring efficiently and successfully, but where there is one Hawaiian, there should be five. 'The harvest is great, but the laborers are few.' How earnestly ought we to pray 'the Lord of the harvest that he will send for the laborers into the harvest.' "

XL.

THE LAST.

We are now brought to the last Paper, concluding the series in which we have endeavored to present a sketch of what we witnessed during our cruise through the Islands of Micronesia. These papers have multiplied beyond our original design, and we now find it more difficult to break off than to continue, but as there must be a "last number," we have concluded that it should be " No. XL."

In bringing these sketches to a close, we are, by no means, inclined to break off our study of the Micronesians and those interesting islands. We hope to have still much pleasant correspondence with the missionaries. If, in future years, circumstances should be favorable, we should not be disinclined to make another trip through that region of the great Pacific, hence we do not say "farewell" to either missionaries or Micronesians.

We think our readers will be interested in glancing over the following catalogue of Micronesian Missionaries :

American Missionaries in Micronesia.

Rev. B. G. Snow and wife, on Strong's Island, or Kusaie, from Oct. 1852, to present date. It is expected that they will remove to Marshall Islands next year, and their station be supplied by Hawaiian Missionaries.

Rev. L. H. Gulick, M. D., and wife, on Ascension, from Sept. 1852, to October 1859—removed to Ebon, and remained there until Oct. 1860, and since that time upon a visit to Hawaiian Islands, now under designation for Gilbert or Kingsmill Islands.

Rev. A. A. Sturges and wife, on Ascension, from September, 1852, to present date. Mrs. Sturges is now visiting Honolulu.

Rev. E. T. Doane and wife, on Ascension, from Feb. 1855, to Oct. 1857, removed in 1857 to Marshall Islands, (Ebon,) and is now there. Mrs. Doane on a visit to Honolulu.

Rev. H. Bingham, jr., and wife, on Apaiang, Gilbert Islands, from Dec. 1857, to present date.

Rev. George Pierson, M.D., and wife, on Strong's Island, from Sept. 1855, to Oct. 1857, and then removed to Ebon, where remained until Oct. 1859. Now settled as Pastor of Presbyterian Church, in Brooklyn, California.

Rev. E. P. Roberts and wife, on Ascension, from Oct. 1858, to July, 1861. Now in California.

Hawaiian Missionaries in Micronesia.

B. Kamikaula and wife. Teachers in Ascension from 1852 to his death, which occurred in 1858. His wife has since been married to H. Aea, the Hawaiian Missionary on Ebon, Marshall Islands.

D. Opunui and wife. He died at Strong's Island, in 1853, and his wife returned to Sandwich Islands.

S. Kamnkahiki, and wife. They went to Ascension, in 1855, as teachers, and returned in 1857. They are now located at Hana on the island of Maui, where he is most usefully employed as a licensed preacher.

J. W. Kanoa and wife. They sailed in company with Rev. Dr. Pierson, in 1855, and were located two years upon Strong's Island, and were then transferred to Apaiang, Gilbert Islands, where they are now actively engaged in the missionary work, associated with the Rev. H. Bingham, jr.

The Rev. J. Mahoe and wife, sailed in 1858, and are now upon the Island of Tarawa, Gilbert Group. They are associated with

K. Haina and wife, who sailed in 1860.

H. Aea and wife sailed in 1860, and are associated with the Rev. Mr. Doane, on Ebon, Marshall Islands.

From the foregoing catalogue, it appears that seven American Missionaries, with their wives, and seven Hawaiians with their wives, are all the laborers who have ever been employed in that missionary field. Whatever of good has been accomplished has been done by them. Four of the American Missionaries and four of the Hawaiians are now connected with that mission. The Rev. Mr. Gulick and family, Mrs. Sturges, and Mrs. Doane, are now visiting the Sandwich Islands, but they are expecting to return. The Hawaiians, who have returned, are not expected to be again employed.

From a careful review of the Micronesian Islands as a field of missionary labor, the number of islands which should be occupied by missionaries, the number of people to whom the gospel should be preached, the success which has attended the work, so far as prosecuted, and the prospects of success, we are fully impressed with the belief that the enterprise should be vigorously carried forward. There are obstacles to be overcome, and difficulties to be encountered, but not greater than are presented in other parts of the world. The low coral islands of the Gilbert or Kingsmill and Marshall groups, are unlike many other missionary fields, but judging from the present prospects, and the success of missionaries upon similar localities in the "South Seas," we may anticipate most happy results. The following statement respecting the success of the English and native missionaries in the "South Seas," upon the coral islands of the Hervey Group, we copy from a recent report of the Rev. J. Bicknell, who has visited Fanning's Island, where many of these natives are employed in the manufacture of cocoanut oil:

The following communication was addressed to Rev. L. Smith, Corresponding Secretary of Hawaiian Missionary Society:

"FANNING'S ISLAND, Sept. 24, 1861.

"Rev. and Dear Sir:

"You are aware that in the month of June last, I took passage from Honolulu in the schooner *Marilda* for this island. The motives which influenced me to make the voyage were these; first to confer with my brother, whom I had not seen for some years second to obtain a knowl edge of the manufacture of cocoanut oil: third, to form an acquaintance with the people of some of the islands of the South·Pacific under the patronage of the London Missionary Society, so as to be informed of the manner of operations of that Society in conducting its missions.

The passage down was made in nine days. Fanning's Island is the first lagoon island I have seen, consequently the sight is an agreeable change. My visit has been a pleasant one, every thing being done on the part of the proprietors of the island to make it so.

Upon my landing, the native operatives (people of Manihiki and Rakahanga, lagoon islands of the South Pacific,) were all assembled on the beach to see the Orometua, or Missionary; word having previously reached the shore that there was one on board.

Unlike the Marquesans, these people I found to be a very mild and inoffensive race. In general appearance they resemble the Tahitians; —their costume and style of civilization being the same. Their language resembles the Rarotongan. Their missionary teachers are from that island; two of them are stationed on Manihiki, and one on Rakahanga. Also, I found upon the island, a few natives from the Paumotu, or Chain Islands. The whole of the native population amounted to about 150, about two-thirds of the number are employed in the manufacture of cocoanut oil. Among these people, there were seventeen church members; a deacon from the church at Manihiki being appointed over them as their spiritual teacher.

Shortly after my arrival, the operatives were paid off, their term of service having expired. On the 17th July, they returned in the *Marilda* to their homes. While they remained on the island, I conducted their religious services, meeting with them three times on the Sabbath, and twice through the week. With the Manihiki and Rakahanga people, I communicated through the Rarotongan language, and with the Paumotuans, through the Tahitian. I found them attentive listeners. Such as had Bibles, brought them to Church, and followed the reading. Those who were furnished with pencil and paper, took notes. One thing which struck me very favorably was this, the whole congregation, both young and old, joined in the singing. As might be expected, there was not very much of music in the singing, but the absence of melody was compensated, however, by the hearty good-will with which all joined in the strain. There was an attractive simplicity in the religious worship of these islanders highly pleasing to behold. Would that the like simplicity would obtain among the more civilized races!

They pressed me very strongly to accompany them to their islands. It would have given me great pleasure to have gone with them, but my state of health, at the time, would not admit of it. I wrote a joint letter, however, to the Missionary brethren bidding them God-speed in their labor of love. Also, I put into the hands of my brother (who was to accompany the people on their return) a paper containing a list of questions to be asked of the Missionary Brethren.

The nature of these questions may be known from the answers to them, the substance of which is as follows:

The mission on Manihiki and Rakahanga was established in 1849. The *John Williams* (missionary bark) has called six times. Two white missionaries have visited the island, Mr. Buzacott, and Mr. Gill. The population of Manihiki is 454, that of Rakahanga 475. The number of church members on Manihiki 137; on Rakahanga 94. The people are governed by Kings, or Chiefs; one on Manihiki, and one on Rakahanga;—the chief of Rakahanga has also an influence on Manihiki. The influence of these chiefs is considerable, (though their power is not absolute as was that of the chiefs of 'Hawaii' in former times.) The missionaries receive no stated salaries—their supplies consist of articles of clothing, &c., contributed by the members of the churches at Rarotonga. The people contribute weekly supplies of food for the maintenance of the missionaries. The state of society is peaceable. The people are governed by laws, which are very strict; being the same as those of Rarotonga. The missionaries exert almost an unbounded influence over the people. The Rarotongan Bible and hymn book, are the devotional books in use. All can read excepting some of the old people. The people are on the increase. They live in villages; the houses being ranged on each side of the road. There are two villages on Manihiki, and one on Rakahanga. On Rakahanga, the houses are, for the most part, built of stone and plastered. The churches are built of stone, of which churches there is one in each village; the dimensions of each being 60 feet long, 36 feet wide and 18 feet on the walls. The people subsist upon cocoanuts and fish;—the islands also produce a species of taro of very inferior quality called by the natives, puroka,— the Tahitian name for it, is Apura. The islands are but seldom visited by whaleships. The people obtain their supplies of clothing from Fanning's Island, as the rewards of their labors in the manufacture of cocoanut oil. In former years, the clothing of these people consisted of matting made from the pandanus leaf; the men wore *maros*, and the women the *pau*, and also the *kihei*. At present, the men are habited in pants and shirts, and the women in loose robes, or gowns.

On the 15th August, the *Marilda* returned from Manihiki, bringing a new band of natives, about 130 in all. Thirty-six of the number being church members.

My intercourse with these people has been of the most pleasing kind. I thank God for granting me the privilege of witnessing the triumphs of His grace among these islanders. I begin now to have a hope of the christianization of all the islands of Polynesia. This work is pre-eminently that of native missionaries. It can be carried on with the aid of only a few foreign ones. Neither is there a necessity to translate the scriptures into all the different dialects, since one translation may suffice for those which are the nearest resembling, as we see in the case of the Rarotongan and Manihiki languages. I see no reason now why the Hawaiian literature may not be introduced into the Marquesas. The resemblance between the Rarotongan and the language of Manihiki, is not very much greater than that between the Hawaiian and the Marquesan.

This shift I believe may be adopted with success, should the means not be at hand for printing the Scriptures in the Marquesan language. I have exercised the Manihiki and Rakahanga people in Bible class, and have found them fluent readers of the Rarotongan Scriptures.

With a little patient instruction, Marquesans may become as equally proficient in the Hawaiian.

The teachers employed among these islanders, seem to be more eminent for their love for souls, than for their learning. The true missionary salt is the unction for souls."

INDEX.